'Oh, Andrew. . .'

Jennifer reached out and touched the blooms with her finger. 'You shouldn't have gone to so much trouble for me ——'

'Pampered, you said. How can you pamper a woman without roses?' His voice was husky and much too close.

The room seemed suddenly very small, his presence filling it, and for the first time she was shockingly, intensely aware of him.

Dear Reader

Margaret O'Neill has written a quartet based around Princes Park Hospital, and CHRISTMAS IS FOREVER launches the four books, which will appear in following months. Poppy works on the paediatric ward, while Jennifer in SECOND THOUGHTS by Caroline Anderson works in Paediatric Outpatients, so plenty of babies and children this festive month! Animals, too, in CELEBRITY VET by Carol Wood, finishing with a Scottish island cottage hospital in CURE FOR HEARTACHE by Patricia Robertson. All home-grown stories to wish you a very merry Christmas.

The Editor

Caroline Anderson's nursing career was brought to an abrupt halt by a back injury, but her interest in medical things led her to work first as a medical secretary, and then, after completing her teacher training, as a lecturer in medical office practice to trainee medical secretaries. In addition to writing, she also runs her own business from her home in rural Suffolk, where she lives with her husband, two daughters, mother and dog.

Recent titles by the same author:

THE SPICE OF LIFE
JUST WHAT THE DOCTOR ORDERED

SECOND THOUGHTS

BY

CAROLINE ANDERSON

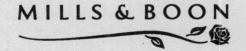

MILLS & BOON LIMITED
ETON HOUSE, 18–24 PARADISE ROAD
RICHMOND, SURREY, TW9 1SR

*First published in Great Britain 1993
by Mills & Boon Limited*

© Caroline Anderson 1993

*Australian copyright 1993
Philippine copyright 1993
This edition 1993*

ISBN 0 263 78378 2

*Set in 10 on 12 pt Linotron Times
03-9312-50428*

*Typeset in Great Britain by Centracet, Cambridge
Made and printed in Great Britain*

CHAPTER ONE

'WOULDN'T it be *nice* to be pampered. . .'

'Pampered?' Andrew flipped the file shut, put the cap on his fountain pen and sat back in his chair, locking his hands behind his head and stretching his long body. 'I suppose it would.' He chuckled. 'I haven't really thought about it. Too busy.'

Jennifer gave a rueful little laugh. 'Mmm — and we're only halfway through. Would you like a cup of tea?'

'Life-saver,' he said with a grin. 'I missed my lunch. Are you having one?'

She chuckled. 'On the sly. If the patients and their parents see me sitting down with a cup in my hand while they wait for another ten minutes I'll be lynched!'

'Messy — bring it in here and we'll tell them we're having a case conference — on second thoughts, bring in the cup and the next patient. It would be nice to get home tonight.'

'My thoughts exactly,' she said with a laugh. 'What is it they call Friday? Poet's Day?'

'Push off early, tomorrow's Saturday.' He snorted. 'Fat chance.'

Jennifer picked up the stack of files and went out into the crowded waiting-room to be greeted by a chorus of dissent from the ranks.

'Sister, are we going to be waiting much longer? We've got people for the weekend and we have to meet them off the train,' one woman asked anxiously.

'Yeah, if we sit here much longer we'll be needing geriatrics, not paediatrics,' a man put in.

She smiled assurance at the bored children and disgruntled parents. 'I'm sorry we've had to keep you so long; Dr Barrett had to deal with an emergency earlier and it's put him back. He'll be with you all as soon as he can.' She gave the secretary the pile of notes and picked up the next few, then went into the kitchen and found one of the domestic staff. 'Beattie, do me a favour, could you? Dr Barrett would love a cup of tea in his office, and I could do with one, but for heaven's sake don't take it out of here!'

'After you, are they?'

Jennifer laughed and tucked an escaping strand of red-brown hair back under her frilly cap. 'Aren't they always? There's a joker out there, too. "We'll be needing geriatrics soon",' she mimicked wickedly. 'Just leave my tea on the side, I'll come and grab it when I can.'

She went back into Andrew's office and handed him the stack of files. 'Here you go. William Griffin first.'

'Ah, right, our little man who's failing to thrive. Let's see what the results turned up.'

They opened the file and pored over the notes. 'Stool, urine and blood cultures all sterile, no blood in the stools, blood chemistry and liver function all normal, and thyroid, and sweat sodium. That rules out thyroid problems or cystic fibrosis, or any nasty liver problems. The serology all looks good — no sign of infection. Did we get a chest X-ray back? And there should have been a barium meal and follow-through.'

'Yes, here we are, here's the radiologist's report.'

Jennifer pulled it out and handed it to him just as Beattie brought in the tea.

'Wonderful, thank you.' He flashed her a grateful smile and slipped it while he frowned at the report. 'Do you know what I think?' he said after a moment. 'I reckon he's got an intussusception.'

'Really? What about the stools? No sign of occult blood, or abdominal pain or vomiting. I know he had diarrhoea, but what about the cough? And the weight loss?'

'That could be due to the anorexia—if he's off his food, he will lose weight. Anyway, the pain and vomiting and bloody stools are typical of acute, not chronic intussuseption. I think we'll have another look, perhaps under sedation. Is there a surgeon we can call down?'

'Yes, I think it's Ross Hamilton today. Shall I get him paged?'

'Not for a bit. I'd like an ultrasound of that bowel, and I'd like to examine him to see if I can feel anything this time. Could you call him for me?'

'Sure.' She popped her head round the door. 'William Griffin, please?'

His mother carried him in, a little boy of two and a half who looked at least fourth months younger.

'Sorry, he's dozed off,' the mother explained.

Andrew smiled apologetically at her. 'I'm sorry I kept you waiting; we had a prem baby at lunchtime that needed my attention. Let him sleep for a minute while you tell me how he's been getting on.'

'Oh, I can see him going downhill in front of my eyes—he's very reluctant to eat, and he's been sick a couple of times now. I'm so worried. . .'

Andrew laid his large hand over hers and squeezed gently. 'Don't fret. We've managed to rule out a lot of very nasty things. There are a couple of other possibilities that I want to eliminate with a few more tests. Has he had any abdominal pain?'

'Once or twice he's complained about tummy-ache, and then a while later he's had diarrhoea.'

Andrew nodded and made a couple of notes. 'I'd like to feel his tummy, but I don't want to wake him if I can avoid it. The more relaxed he is, the more I can feel. Do you think you could lay him down in your arms so I can try?'

She shifted carefully, and William made a tiny noise and remained asleep.

'He's out for the count, isn't he?' Andrew chuckled softly. 'OK, let's see what we can feel.'

He eased up the little T-shirt, slipped the shorts down a fraction and very gently and carefully made a minute inspection of the whole abdomen. After a moment he returned to the upper right quadrant, and then pulled the T-shirt back down and looked up at the mother.

'Right, I'd like him to have an ultrasound scan of his tummy. Did you have one when you were pregnant?'

She nodded.

'So you know it doesn't hurt at all—in fact, he's so drowsy he might not even know he'd had it done. Sister will give you directions to that department, and then when we've got the result I'll see you again. All right?' Handing her the completed request form, he smiled reassuringly. 'Give this to the receptionist in the ultrasound department.'

Mrs Griffin stood up carefully, cradling William

against her chest, and Jennifer showed her out, directed her to Ultrasound and went back in.

'You found something.'

'Mmm. A soft mass, nothing specific. Could well be a small section of ileum intruding into the colon. Then again, it might not.'

'So what else could it be? A tumour?'

'Could be. Let's hope not. We won't know, I don't suppose, until we open him up. As soon as he comes back I'd like Ross Hamilton down here, I think.'

She nodded. 'Will do. Who's next?'

He glanced at the file. 'The Robinson triplets.'

'You won't recognise them. They're huge!'

He grinned. 'Good! We could do with a happy ending.'

She called Mr and Mrs Robinson and their three delightful little baby girls, who had been born prematurely at thirty weeks. Now almost five months, they were definitely thriving!

'Oh, let me help you,' Jennifer said with a smile, and took one of the babies from the mother. 'Now, who's this?'

The mother peered at her. 'Megan.'

'Right, come on, Megan, let's go and see that nice Dr Barrett.' The baby beamed at her, and made a grab for her pens in the top pocket. 'Oh, no you don't!' she laughed. 'Come on, madam.'

She led the little group through into Andrew's consulting-room and watched while he greeted the whole family with his warm enthusiasm. The babies had been in his care since birth, and for a long time their grip on life had seemed fragile to say the least. Then, one by one, they grew stronger, but the smallest, Megan, had still been troubled by a slight chestiness for some time, and Andrew had felt it advisable to monitor them for three months after their discharge. Now, his delight reflected the depth of his concern in their early days.

'Oh, well, I don't have to lay a finger on them to tell they're doing magnificently!' he said, but nevertheless he inspected each one with great care, and asked endless questions about their developmental progress, feeding problems and so on. Megan's chest appeared to have resolved itself, and Andrew declared himself well satisfied. 'I should say they're only about three weeks behind now, which is excellent! Give them a bit longer and you would never have known. Well, I think we can safely discharge you young ladies from our care now,' he said to the babies, and they all gurgled on cue.

'Heartbreakers, all of them,' he said with a laugh, and, after answering the parents' last few questions, he showed them out with almost visible reluctance.

'If I didn't know better I'd think you'd grown attached to those little girls,' Jennifer teased.

'Me — would I?' he said innocently. 'Right, who's next?

The clinic proceeded without any hitches, and shortly before they finished little William Griffin and his mother returned to the department.

They called Ross Hamilton down, and he arrived just as they dealt with the last patient.

They called Mrs Griffin in after Andrew had filled Ross in on the results to date and examined the ultrasound image. There was an indistinct but abnormal mass shown on the picture, and after examining

William Ross agreed with Andrew that it was most likely an intussusception.

They explained the implications to Mrs Griffin, and told her that he would need surgery as soon as was reasonable. Ross glanced at his watch. 'Well, it's getting on to do anything today. Can we admit him now and go for tomorrow morning? I'd rather have lab staff around.'

Andrew nodded, understanding his unspoken thoughts. If it proved to be a tumour rather than the loop of bowel tucked inside itself that they thought it was, then they would need biopsies and frozen sections and tissue analysis to determine further treatment. It was important to have the full backup of all necessary staff, and they were more likely to be available during the day. Also, while a minor delay would make no difference at all to William, it would give the parents time to prepare him — and themselves — for the operation and his stay in hospital.

'Right, Mrs Griffin, can you take him home, give him a light supper and bring him back by seven this evening, and we'll sort him out tomorrow morning. Is that OK?'

She nodded, and Ross went back to his ward, leaving Mrs Griffin looking worried. 'Will I be able to stay with him?'

'Oh, yes — he's far too young to leave. He'll need you around, if you can possibly manage it.'

'How long will he be in?'

'A few days — a week at the most. Is that a problem?'

She shook her head, and after a few more questions Jennifer gave her a leaflet about the paediatric unit and what she would need to bring, and showed her out.

When she went back into Andrew's office, he was just closing the file.

'And another week bites the dust,' he said with weary good humour.

She returned his smile. 'Time flies when you're enjoying yourself.'

The clinic secretary tapped on the door and came in. 'Can I have the files, Dr Barrett?'

'Sure. Here we are, the last few. I'm admitting William Griffin, so his file needs to go up to the ward.'

'I'll pop it in on my way out. Have a good weekend.'

'Thanks, Janet. You too.'

'Uh-huh. Bye, Sister. See you on Monday.'

'No doubt,' Jennifer said with a little sigh as the door closed behind the secretary. A tiny yawn escaped her, and she laughingly apologised.

'Tired?'

She nodded. 'Aren't I always? Friday's a killer, isn't it? The clinic always seems endless.'

'Never mind, you've got the weekend to look forward to.'

'Mmm.'

'You don't sound very convinced.'

She picked up the blanket on the examination couch and refolded it, hugging it against her chest. 'Oh, I just wish it could be different for once. To have someone say, "Come on, drop everything, I'm going to take you away from it all" — wouldn't that be wonderful?'

'Is it really so grim?'

She sighed and put the blanket down. 'No. Now I'm sounding like a spoilt brat, and I don't mean to. It's just that I know that in company with X million other working women I'll have to clean the flat and do the washing and wrestle with Tim's homework and repair his uniform, and it would be nice if, just now and again, it could be different. . .'

Andrew frowned at her. 'When did you last get away?'

She blinked. 'Me? Heavens, I don't remember. Tim went to his father in July for a week, and I had that fortnight off to be with him in August, but I haven't been away for years.' She laughed a little self-consciously. 'I don't think I'd know how to relax now if I had the chance.'

Andrew stood up slowly and took his jacket off the back of the chair, shrugging into it thoughtfully.

'What are you doing this weekend?'

She looked up at him, all six foot three of warm brown eyes and gentle smile, and wondered if he'd gone suddenly deaf.

'Cleaning the flat, doing the washing——'

'What else? Anything you can't just drop?'

She tipped her head on one side and her brows twitched together in a little frown. 'No—not that I can think of. Why?'

He hesitated, then seemed to make up his mind. 'How do you fancy being pampered?'

She felt her jaw drop slightly. 'What?'

'I wondered if you'd like to come out to the cottage for the weekend.'

It was totally unexpected, and Jennifer floundered. Oh, sure, they'd had the odd drink together after work, but the weekend? 'Um—I don't think—I mean, Tim——'

Andrew flushed slightly. 'I don't want you to miscon-strue my invitation. I just thought you and Tim might benefit from a weekend in the country, but if you'd rather not please say so. I don't want to embarrass you.'

She looked away, suddenly feeling foolish. Of course he wasn't suggesting a weekend of unbridled sex. Heavens, the very idea! If there was one thing Andrew Barrett wasn't, it was a ladies' man. He was also painfully honest, with himself and everybody else. If he had meant to seduce her, he would have made it perfectly clear. As it was, he had made it perfectly clear that he *didn't*. And anyway, they would have Tim as a chaperon. Not quite sure if the flicker of something she felt was disappointment or relief, she looked back at him.

He was packing up the things on his desk, tidying everything neatly away.

'Andrew?'

He glanced up.

'I—that would be lovely, but I really do have to the washing——'

'Bring it with you. What time would you like me to pick you up?'

She blinked. 'Bring it?'

'Bring it. What time? Seven?

She shook her head dazedly. 'Seven?' She glanced at her watch. Quarter to six. She would just have time to collect Tim and pack a bag. 'Yes, that would be fine—thanks. Are you sure——?'

'Quite sure.' His smile was warmly reassuring and she relaxed.

'We'll be ready.'

* * *

The four-wheel-drive off-roader suited him, Jennifer decided. Big, rugged and capable, devoid of frills but immensely practical.

He loaded their few things and the bag of washing into the back, buckled Tim in safely and held the door for her with quiet courtesy while she climbed up into the front passenger seat. It was quite a step and she was glad she had opted for jeans and not a skirt, although she was sure Andrew wouldn't even have noticed. She had let her hair down and brushed it out, but the layers looked a little ragged unless she finger-dried it upside down, and there hadn't been time between collecting Tim from the childminder and Andrew arriving to pick them up. She found time, though, for a quick swipe of lipstick, more for her self-respect than any attempt at glamour. After all, it wasn't going to be that sort of weekend.

One thing was certain, they were going to eat, if the carrier bags in the back were any indication. He had obviously been shopping since she last saw him, and she had a twinge of guilt that they were causing him a lot of bother — it went with the twinge about ducking out of the housework, and she chewed her lip.

He must have read her mind, because he threw her a teasing grin. 'Just lie back and relax,' he instructed firmly. 'No fretting about the housework. It'll still be there when you go back.'

She laughed without humour. 'Isn't it always?'

'Without fail — like the weeds. They grow regardless of whether I've got time to pull them up.' He turned and winked at Tim over his shoulder. 'OK back there?'

Tim nodded.

'Good. Do you like cats?'

'Oh, yes — I think so.'

'Pets aren't allowed in our flats, so he doesn't get to see all that many animals,' Jennifer explained.

'No? What a shame. I've got two cats — I used to have just one but a week ago this other cat turned up and just adopted us. Bit of a problem, really; it seems she's going to have kittens, and I don't know if Blu-Tack is going to like it.'

'Blu-Tack?'

'Mmm. The other cat. He's a Russian Blue — beautiful pedigree cat, but he's only got three legs. He lost the other one in an accident and the owners didn't want him any more. He's lived with me for two years, two bachelors together, and now we've been invaded.' He laughed briefly. 'It's a little odd.'

She felt suddenly uncomfortable, unsure if he was referring to them or just the pregnant cat. Well, too bad, she thought. He had invited them, and Tim was so excited by the thought of going away for the weekend with her that there was no way she was going to spoil it by being petty. She would just have to make sure they didn't get in Andrew's way.

It was nearly half-past seven by the time they arrived, and the last rays of the September sun were gilding the cottage, sparkling on the latticed windows and setting fire to the riot of flowers that flanked the soft pink walls.

'Oh, Andrew, it's lovely!' she exclaimed, enchanted.

He gave a dry chuckle. 'You're definitely seeing at its best. In the winter without the roses and the perennials it can look a bit bare, and it's sometimes a bit draughty inside if the wind gets up. Still, I like it.

Here, Tim, take the key and go and open the door for your mother, there's a good chap.'

He opened the back of the car and picked up four shopping bags, and ushered Jennifer into the cottage. 'Go and sit down—make yourself at home. I'll bring the shopping in then make some tea.'

'I could make the tea——'

'No. Sit down.'

'But——'

'No buts. Pampered, you said, and pampered it's going to be. Sit.'

Overruled, she gave him a tiny smile and surrendered. 'Yes, sir.'

She followed the wave of his arm and went through into a cosy little sitting-room, heavily beamed and furnished with affection. There was nothing even remotely designerish about it, from the elderly chair covers to the faded velvet curtains and the worn rug in front of the old inglenook fireplace, but it was unbelievably homely.

There was a chair that was obviously his, pulled up near the fire with a remote-control unit on an old oak table beside it. A large grey cat with unblinking emerald-green eyes stared at her from its depths, then tucked his nose in his paws again and went back to sleep. Blu-Tack, obviously.

She chose the chair on the other side of the fireplace and sat down, almost vanishing into its welcome embrace.

Bliss. She kicked off her shoes, tucked her tired feet up under her bottom and fell instantly asleep.

* * *

He was quite surprised at how right she looked, sitting curled up in the other chair with her head resting on one hand like that. Her wrist was bent, so he carefully eased her arm down and replaced it with a cushion.

It didn't disturb her. Her grey eyes fluttered open for a second, she made a funny little noise and snuggled further down, and then was still again.

Andrew scooped Blu-Tack off the chair opposite and settled himself into it, the cat on his lap, and touched the remote control. Soft music flooded the room, and he rested his head back and relaxed, content to watch her sleep.

There was something strangely intimate about it that touched him, deep inside. It surprised him, just as her rightness here had surprised him.

He hadn't meant to issue the invitation. It was quite out of character, but perhaps it was time to break out a little. Oh, true, he'd taken her out for the occasional drink, but he'd never kissed her goodnight — unless you counted a peck on her sweetly scented cheek. He supposed it was in part a reluctance to disturb the balance of their working relationship, a relationship that had meant a great deal to him in the six months since he had taken up his consultancy.

The children's outpatients sister was one of the most important people on the team, and he had come to rely very heavily on her. Apart from her background knowledge of many of the patients, her gentle efficiency and firm kindness had to be seen to be believed. She would be a wonderful mother — *was* a wonderful mother, he corrected himself, thinking of the serious, intelligent but delightful child asleep upstairs.

While Jennifer dozed, he had cooked Tim a prawn

omelette with salad and a microwaved jacket potato — Tim's choice. Another surprise. Andrew had been quite prepared to do fish fingers and beans and chips, but the child had looked doubtful — not rude enough to decline, but definitely not enthusiastic. Andrew had asked him to choose, given him a list of possibilities and that was what he'd selected.

'We don't have chips and things like that at home,' Tim had told him guilelessly. 'Only when I go out for the weekend with Dad. I don't like them much.'

Interesting. Andrew had filed it for future reference. Likewise the business of the bath.

'Do you usually have a bath before you go to bed?' he'd asked.

'Mum always makes me. Dad doesn't.'

'I think you'd better have one, then,' Andrew had said, and put that in the file, too.

After Andrew tucked him into bed in the little room overlooking the orchard, he had left him reading for a little while and gone downstairs to prepare a meal for himself and Jennifer. When he'd gone back up half an hour later, Tim was asleep, his book still in his hand.

Andrew had looked at it and was surprised at how advanced it was, well beyond Tim's seven years. He stroked the soft brown hair back off his little brow, tucked the quilt in round his slight shoulders and then turned down the light, leaving a soft glow in case he woke. Then he had gone down to Jennifer.

As he watched her sleep, a curious contentment stole over him, together with a touch of regret because he knew that when they went back the house would seem empty. For now, however, it was just exactly right, and he would enjoy the moment and let tomorrow take care of itself.

Jennifer woke to soft lights and the haunting sound of a flute — and pins and needles in her right foot.

She straightened up and blinked. 'Oh — you shouldn't have let me sleep,' she said, embarrassed.

'You were tired.'

'But Tim——'

'Tim's in bed. He's had supper and a bath, and he's out for the count.'

She dropped her head back against the chair. 'Oh. Thank you. You shouldn't have done all that.'

'I'm pampering you, remember?'

His smile was kindly teasing. She returned it, then winced as the circulation came back into her foot.

'Pins and needles?' he guessed, and she nodded, wriggling it. He turned the cat off his knee and crouched in front of her, taking her foot in his large, warm hands and massaging it gently.

'Ow,' she mumbled.

'Hell, isn't it? How's that?'

She felt suddenly uncomfortable with this big man kneeling at her feet.

'Better, thank you,' she told him and almost snatched it out of his hands, further embarrassed by the growl from her stomach.

'Hungry?' he asked with a smile.

'Apparently.' She laughed a little awkwardly.

'Supper's ready when you are. There's a cloakroom at the bottom of the stairs if you want to freshen up.'

She looked dreadful, she thought as she looked at herself in the mirror. Her hair was tousled, her cheeks were flushed and crumpled from the cushion and she looked — wanton was the nearest she could come up with, and it unsettled her.

She splashed her face with cold water and went back into the big farmhouse-style kitchen, where Andrew was just setting the huge old refectory table.

'OK?'

She nodded, avoiding his eyes. 'Can I do anything?'

'Eat,' he said with a grin.

It was no hardship. The meal was wonderful, a seafood concoction with mushrooms and a delicious creamy sauce under the lightest, fluffiest mashed potato she had ever tasted. It was served with fresh sprouting broccoli and glazed carrots, both homegrown, he told her.

'Where did you learn to cook like that?' she asked him, replete, as she sat at the table under orders not to move and watched him clear up.

He laughed. 'Self-defence. I can't stand canteen food and I can't afford a housekeeper. Anyway, I enjoy it. Coffee?'

'Mmm. Can I — ?'

'No. Go and sit down, I'll be with you in a tick.'

'Actually, I think I'll go up and check on Tim, if you really don't need my help.'

'Top of the stairs, turn left and follow your nose. He's in the little bedroom at the end.'

'OK.' She ran lightly up the stairs, noticing as she went the higgledy-piggledy collection of pictures on the walls, etchings and pen and ink drawings and little watercolours, the occasional photograph, an oil on wood. There was no theme, except perhaps the straightforward one of personal choice, pictures collected for no better reason than that he liked them. And what better reason was there?

She found Tim, his cheek cradled on his hand, fast asleep in a wonderful old captain's bed, the forerunner by some hundred years of the modern chipboard equivalent. His lashes dark against his pale cheeks, he looked terribly vulnerable and very small. He also looked as if he belonged in this room, with its distinctly *Boys' Own* flavour.

She brushed a kiss on his cheek, whispered 'Goodnight,' and tiptoed out.

'OK?'

She jumped slightly. Big as he was, she hadn't heard him approach. 'Yes, he's fine. Where did you get that wonderful bed?'

'The bed? It used to be mine when I was a child. I couldn't bear to part with it when my parents died. Obviously I couldn't keep everything, but that I refused to get rid of.' He pushed open a door. 'I've put you in here next to him,' Andrew told her, ushering her in.

It was a delightful room, with high twin beds and pretty lace bedspreads. Her suitcase was lying on one of the beds, and on the table between them was a small vase of roses.

'Oh, Andrew. . .' She reached out and touched the blooms with her finger. 'You shouldn't have gone to so much trouble for me ——'

'Pampered, you said. How can you pamper a woman without roses?' His voice was husky and much too close.

The room seemed suddenly very small, his presence filling it, and for the first time she was shockingly, intensely aware of him.

'Thank you,' she murmured a little breathlessly, and after a second's hesitation he turned and ducked under the doorway.

'Coffee's ready when you are. I'll see you downstairs,' he told her, and she wasn't sure if his voice was a little strained or if she had imagined it.

When she went back down, though, she decided she had imagined it because he was all quiet courtesy and the perfect host. The pregnant black and white cat made herself at home on his lap for a while, and he sat and absently fiddled with her ears while they talked about the children they had seen in the clinic that afternoon.

'We shouldn't be talking shop—you're supposed to be getting away from it all,' he said after a while.

'Do you ever truly get away? Especially with paediatrics. It's rather like being a vet, all those great big trusting eyes. They do something to your insides.'

He laughed. 'And you accused me of getting attached to the Robinsons!'

'Well, they are delicious,' she said with a forgiving smile.

'Mmm. They're very lucky people. And unlike most parents, they realise it. Probably because they had such a struggle before IVF finally gave them their family. Most people just take their children for granted.'

Jennifer nodded and sighed. 'It's easy, though, isn't it? I just wish Tim meant more to his father.'

'Why did you get divorced?' Andrew asked quietly.

She shrugged. 'Who knows? Nick decided one day that he couldn't handle the responsibility any more, and he went. Crazy, really. We'd got through his house years when he was never at home—perhaps that was it? Perhaps once he reached the point where he was at home more, he realised we weren't what he wanted. Whatever, he left. He's always been very good about helping financially, though. Whatever his other failings, he's always been meticulous about that. Well, he is meticulous. Everything always has to be just so. He'd rip this room apart and re-do it all, because it's not perfect.'

Andrew glanced round, and shrugged. 'I know it's not up to much, but I like it.'

She flushed, mortified. 'Sorry, that was unbelievably tactless, but I really didn't mean it like it sounded. It's just that Nick's taste is — well, let's say clinical, shall we? And I became so indoctrinated that now I can't seem to make our flat homely, but this house — I think it's charming, restful, cosy. . .everything a home should be. I don't know quite how you've done it, but I love it and I think it would be a great shame to change it.'

'Thank you.' They exchanged smiles, and he tipped the cat off his lap and stood up. 'Nightcap?'

'No, thanks. Actually, I'm ready for bed.'

She stood up and went over to him, reaching up to kiss him lightly on the cheek. 'Thank you for spoiling us. You're a good man.'

He flushed slightly and squeezed her shoulders. 'You deserve it. You're a lovely girl, you should have someone spoiling you all the time.'

She laughed. 'Oh, no, I'd get fat and lazy. I'm better off as I am. Goodnight.'

For a second she thought he was going to kiss her, but then his hands slid down her arms and he stepped back. 'See you in the morning.'

She climbed the picture-lined staircase and checked Tim, then washed and climbed into bed, snuggling down against the freshly scented linen with a contented sigh. She was asleep in seconds.

CHAPTER TWO

JENNIFER woke to the sounds of the countryside — birdsong, barking dogs, the rusty squawk of a pheasant, and in the distance the drone of a tractor. She smiled to herself. In a strange way it was noisier than the town!

She stretched lazily and glanced at her watch, then threw back the covers, horrified. Ten to nine! What on earth would Andrew think of her, lying in this late?

She pushed her feet into slippers and was reaching for her dressing-gown when there was a tap on the door.

'Jennifer?'

She pushed her arms hastily into the robe and opened the door, overwhelmingly conscious of her tousled hair and flushed cheeks.

Andrew was standing there, dressed in soft old cords and a plaid shirt open at the neck, balancing a tray on one large hand. His hair was still damp from the shower, and one unruly lock had fallen forwards over his brow. She clenched her fists, shocked at the sudden urge to smooth it back.

'Morning,' she mumbled.

'Morning. Did you sleep all right?'

She ran a hand through her hair, tousling it further. 'Wonderfully, thank you. . .'

He grinned. 'I've brought you breakfast. Tim said you only ever have tea and toast, but I thought maybe

I could tempt you with a boiled egg from one of the little bantams.'

He set the tray down on the bedside table. There was a cup of tea, a slice of wholemeal toast and a tiny, perfect little brown egg in a miniature eggcup. And a yellow rosebud, just on the point of opening.

'You really are taking this to extremes, aren't you?' she said shakily.

'Of course. You deserve it—I've been working you too hard. In you get.'

He held the bedclothes so that she had no choice but to kick off her slippers and get back into bed. She felt incredibly foolish and terribly spoilt.

'Relax and enjoy,' he advised, and set the tray down on her lap. 'We'll be in the garden when you're ready. Why don't you have another little sleep?'

'Oh, I couldn't,' she protested, but after she had eaten the little egg and the slice of toast and drunk the delicately flavoured tea, she found she had no urge to get up. 'Just a few minutes,' she said to herself, and setting the tray down, she snuggled back under the covers and fell instantly asleep.

The next time she woke it was to the sound of a motor much closer than before, and much higher pitched. Throwing back the bedclothes, she crossed over to the window and looked out, to see Tim sitting on a tiny red tractor, going up and down the garden with Andrew striding beside him, occasionally reaching across to turn the steering-wheel slightly. They both looked perfectly content, so she took her time washing and dressing before she went downstairs, intending to clear up the kitchen and look around for something for lunch.

She found the kitchen immaculate, a quiche browning gently in the oven, and a pile of washing folded on the table.

She did a mild double-take. Her clothes? And Tim's?

She sat down slowly, gratitude warring with embarrassment. The thought of anyone else — especially a man, and particularly her boss! — going through her washing was enough to bring her out in a rash. All that ancient underwear. . .

She gave a low moan and put her face in her hands. How was she ever going to face him again?

'Jennifer? Are you feeling all right?'

'Yes — no,' she mumbled, and forced herself to look up at him. 'You shouldn't have done my washing,' she said firmly.

He grinned. 'All part of the service, ma'am. I'm afraid it isn't ironed, but I'm not much good at that; I tend to burn things. Coffee?'

She sighed and gave up. 'Thank you, that would be lovely. Where's Tim?'

'Out in the garden, molesting Blu-Tack.'

'Is he all right?'

He raised an eyebrow at her anxious tone. 'Which one? I believe they'll both survive the encounter.'

She smiled. 'I meant was Blu-Tack all right with children. Some cats can be a bit funny.'

Andrew shrugged. 'He's a little shy, but he's very friendly once he knows you. I've never known him scratch anyone yet, and my sister's children persecute him mercilessly. Mummy-cat's taken herself off somewhere, though. Bit too much for her, all this attention.' He handed her a mug of coffee. 'We've just cut the grass.'

'I know — I watched you from the window. Tim will have enjoyed it.'

'Kids always do. I get through gallons of petrol when I have little visitors.' He settled himself at the table, his broad shoulders straining the soft fabric of his plaid shirt. The mug almost vanished in his big hands. He looked at her thoughtfully. 'I have to nip in to the hospital for a little while to see William Griffin. It was an ileocolic intussusception, by the way, and Ross said he sorted it out without any trouble, but I'd just like to have a look. I thought we could go for a walk after lunch if you feel up to it.'

She laughed. 'Andrew, I'm not ill, just a bit tired. Where did you want to go?'

'In the woods. There's a badger's sett and a couple of foxholes, and endless rabbit holes. I thought Tim would like it, but you could stay here if you'd rather.'

'No, that would be great. I'm sure he'll love it, but have you got time?'

He looked surprised. 'Of course — this is your weekend, Jennifer. Stop feeling guilty and enjoy it.'

So she did. Lunch was superb, the walk a delight, brought to life by Andrew's extensive knowledge of the countryside. Tim, who was fascinated by all knowledge, soaked it up like a sponge, and Jennifer strolled behind, content simply to watch them interact.

If only his father was like that with him, she thought, and felt a twinge of sadness. Nick had never understood Tim, and the older he got, the wider the gulf seemed to grow.

Not that Nick's casual attitude to access exactly helped, although recently he had been better, making more of an effort not to break arrangements, but often when Tim came back he was silent and uncommunicative, and Nick always seemed to heave a sigh of relief when he handed him over to her again.

'Penny for them.'

She looked up into Andrew's homely, lived-in face. He would understand, but it seemed disloyal to discuss Nick's attitude with him. She felt she had already said too much last night.

Instead she smiled. 'Sorry, I was miles away.'

'Hey, Andrew, look at this!' Tim called excitedly.

With a last, searching glance at her face, Andrew turned back to Tim and the huge bracket fungus he had found.

That evening, after they had eaten supper and while she put Tim to bed, Andrew cleared up the kitchen and then lit the fire in the little sitting-room. It had been a glorious, sunny September day, but with the clear sky came a sharp drop in temperature, sufficient justification, Andrew said smilingly, for the self-indulgence of a log fire.

He had opened a bottle of Australian Cabernet with supper, and they finished it off, sitting in their respective chairs in companionable silence and gazing into the flames, while the pure, clear sound of a chorister flowed around them.

Jennifer laid her head back against the chair and closed her eyes, letting it all wash over her.

'This is beautiful,' she murmured.

'You aren't really in the right place — you should be here for the best image.'

She laughed drowsily. 'But you're there.'

His voice was soft. 'You could always join me.'

And because she was so relaxed and perhaps a little tipsy, and because he was so comfortable to be with, it seemed perfectly natural to go over to him and settle herself on his lap, her head against his broad shoulder, and close her eyes again.

'Better?' he asked quietly, and she made a small sound of agreement.

'This is lovely — what is it?'

'The "Pie Jesu", from Fauré's *Requiem*.'

'It's so peaceful — uplifting, spiritual.'

'Requiem means rest,' he told her, and she sighed softly and let the music soothe her.

After a while the *Requiem* ended, and she lay cradled on his lap with only the hiss of the logs and the occasional screech of an owl to break the silence.

She could hear the steady thud of his heart, and the slow, even sound of his breathing. His big, blunt hand lay warmly on her knee, and the other arm was around her shoulders, holding her against his solid chest. She opened her eyes and found him looking at her, his expression sober.

'What is it?' she asked softly.

He hesitated for a moment, then murmured, 'I was just wondering if it would ruin everything if I kissed you.'

Her breath lodged in her throat. Unable to reply, she lifted her hand and touched it lightly to his cheek. He had shaved and changed before supper, but even so she could feel the slight rasp of stubble against her palm. She slid her hand round and threaded her fingers through his hair, then gently drew his face down towards hers.

In the moment before their lips met, she wondered

briefly why it had taken them so long to reach this point.

After that, there was no more coherent thought. His lips were firm but gentle, not the clever, practised lips of the master-seducer but hesitant at first, as if it was a long time since he had kissed anybody. Then with a small sound of satisfaction his hand slid up into her hair and steadied her, as if he had remembered what to do, so that when she whimpered and parted her lips he was there, his tongue stroking the velvet recesses of her mouth, drawing her own into his mouth to suckle it gently until she whimpered again.

He shifted her in his arms so that his hands were free, and as he unfastened the buttons on her blouse she could see they were trembling. Then he drew the edges apart and gazed at her, at the soft swell of her breasts above the lace edges of her bra, the rose-pink nipples peaking against the restraint, aching for his attention.

His fingers shook as they brushed the delicate skin, then they moved to the clasp.

'Let me look at you,' he whispered, and nothing had ever seemed more right.

He fumbled the clasp and in the end she helped him, unable to bear the sweet suspense. Her breasts spilled out into his hands and he groaned deep in his throat.

'So lovely,' he whispered, and then his head lowered and his lips and tongue took the place of his fingers, soothing the aching peaks and yet driving them to even greater frenzy. He drew a nipple into his mouth and sucked hard, and with a shocked cry she arched against him.

He lifted his head instantly, his eyes heavy-lidded, dazed. 'Did I hurt you? I'm sorry ——'

'No — no, it was — I want to touch you, too. . .'

Her fingers fumbled with the buttons of his shirt, and he tried to help her but his own hands were shaking nearly as badly. Finally the buttons gave way and she dragged the shirt out of his waistband and slid her arms round his sides as he eased her up against his chest, driving the breath from her lungs in a ragged sigh. The soft scatter of hair chafed unbearably against her sensitive nipples, making them ache for more, and she moved against him restlessly, dragging an answering sigh from his lips as they moved against her shoulder.

'Touch me,' he muttered unevenly, and, unable to resist the invitation, her hands slid up and round, over the smooth skin of his shoulders and down the strong column of his back, then round the sides and over the washboard of his stomach and up, feeling his body shudder beneath his hands, her fingers threading into the lightly tangled curls that clustered in the centre of his chest.

Under her palms she could feel his heart thundering, the blood bounding in his veins. Sliding her hands up over his shoulders, she drew him back to her and lifted her face to his.

His mouth found hers with unerring accuracy, their tongues meshing, wild now with need, and he shifted her again so that he was lying half across her, one leg over hers, the imprint of his arousal hard against her hip.

He ran his hand up her thigh and over her other hip, drawing her harder against him, and his shuddering sigh mingled with hers and was lost in their kiss.

His hand moved again, over the inside of her thigh and up, his palm hot through the fabric of her jeans, cradling the unbearable ache that was building deep inside her.

She arched against him, his name a plea on her lips, and his deep, harsh groan answered her.

Then his hand moved, slowly now, up her side to her shoulders, and he lifted his head and looked deep into her eyes.

'We mustn't,' he whispered, his voice tortured, and she whimpered and moved against him, beyond reason.

'No, love, stop,' he pleaded gruffly.

She reached up and touched his cheek with a trembling hand, his agony finally penetrating the fog of sensation that surrounded her. 'What is it?'

He tipped back his head and groaned, his throat working. There was a dull flush lying over his cheeks, and his breathing was laboured and untidy. 'I hadn't intended — I never meant to go so far. Forgive me.'

'Not if you stop now,' she murmured huskily.

He groaned again, as if he was in pain. 'Jennifer, I have to.'

'No — '

'Yes. I didn't mean this to happen — '

'Neither did I, but it has. . .'

'No it hasn't, not yet, and it isn't going to — not unless you want to end up pregnant.'

She was shocked into stillness. 'Oh, Lord. How unbelievably irresponsible — I didn't even think of that. . .'

His chuckle was wry. 'Neither did I — at least, not in time to do anything about it. Believe me, when I invited you for this weekend, nothing was further from

my mind.' His hands lingering regretfully, he re-
fastened her bra, then drew the edges of her blouse
together again with fingers that were not quite steady.

'Perhaps it's just as well,' he said quietly. 'I wouldn't
want you to wake up in the morning hating me.'

'I could never hate you,' she murmured, and laid her
hand against his heart. It was still pounding, although
more slowly, and he was still clearly aroused. The kind
thing to do would be to get off his lap and go to bed,
leaving him to cool off alone.

But she didn't want to leave him, not when her body
was still singing with need in the aftermath of his
lovemaking. Reaching out her hand, she laid it against
his chest.

'Put the *Requiem* on again,' she said softly.

He reached for the remote control, and the cool,
pure notes poured over them like balm. She settled
herself against his shoulder, her hand on his heart, and
let the tension slowly seep away.

Lord, but she was lovely. Her body was soft against
his, relaxed in sleep, and as he gazed down at her he
remembered the way she had clung to him, the soft
whimpers and little cries of ecstasy she had made.

How he had stopped he would never know, but he
had found the strength from somewhere, and now he
was profoundly glad. He would never have forgiven
himself if she had ended up hating him, but it had just
happened so naturally. It had felt so — *right*, as if their
bodies belonged together.

The *Requiem* ended, the final notes dying away in
the silence, and he lifted her carefully in his arms and
carried her up the stairs to her room.

He debated leaving her clothes on, and decided that a little more self-control would be good for him. He removed them, careful not to wake her, and slipped her under the covers. He left her underwear, however, partly for her dignity and partly because he felt he had played with fire long enough and his self-control was getting singed round the edges.

Shutting the bathroom door, he turned on the shower and stripped, stepping into the scalding water with resignation. There was no point in even trying a cold shower. It would take the combined melt waters of both polar icecaps to cool him off tonight, with Jennifer lying almost naked just feet away from him. With a low growl of frustration, he dropped his head forwards against the tiles and let the hot water stream over him while his body throbbed and ached and called him a fool.

Sunday was another glorious day. For Jennifer it started, like Saturday, with breakfast in bed, this time accompanied by the feather-soft brush of his lips on hers and a husky 'good morning' to wake her.

'We've had a population explosion in the night,' he told her softly. 'Tim and I are in the kitchen — come on down in a minute and see.'

She obediently ate her breakfast while she puzzled over the fact that she was in her underwear. She hadn't been that drunk, surely? She could remember — her cheeks flushed, and she groaned. Had she gone to sleep and he'd carried her to bed? Oh, well, it could have been worse, at least she'd had decent underwear on — not that her underwear was any surprise to him after doing her washing.

She groaned again, and then, pulling on her dressing-gown, made her way downstairs.

Tim was sitting on the floor by the airing cupboard, his eyes like saucers, and on a pile of once-clean sheets the black and white cat who had adopted Andrew reclined with her four tiny little kittens.

'Oh, aren't they adorable?' she breathed. They were all different colours; ginger, black, tortoiseshell and white, and black and white like her.

'We mustn't touch them or she might eat them,' Tim warned her seriously. 'Especially as she doesn't know us very well.'

'Perhaps we'd better let her have some peace now,' Andrew suggested. 'I'll put the top sheet in a box and put them all back in it in a minute.'

Jennifer straightened up and met his eyes. 'Six cats?'

He groaned and laughed softly. 'Don't.'

She smiled. 'You're just an old softie, aren't you?'

'That's me. Why don't you go and wallow in the bath for a while and Tim and I can make her a box and see if we can get her to eat something?'

In fact, the whole day revolved around the cat. They went out to give her peace, then came back to give her food, then went out again for another walk to give her more peace. Finally, at five, he took them home, complete with washing, homework done, and feeling more spoilt and pampered then she had ever felt in her life. He refused her offer of a cup of tea, saying he wanted to check on William Griffin again, so they said their farewells at her door.

'We've had a wonderful weekend,' she told him. 'Thank you.' And she stood on tiptoe and pressed a kiss to his cheek.

'Thank you for having me,' Tim said spontaneously. 'I've had a lovely time — look after the kittens.'

'I will,' Andrew assured him gravely. 'We must do it again.

'Next weekend?' Tim asked hopefully.

'No, I'm sorry, I have to go away next weekend.'

'And you're with your father, Tim,' Jennifer reminded him.

Andrew said, 'Someday soon, though. We'll sort something out, perhaps one day after school. OK?'

Tim nodded enthusiastically. 'Can I feed the hens again?'

Andrew tousled his hair and hugged him to his side briefly. 'Of course.' He looked up at Jennifer. 'Take care. I'll see you tomorrow.'

She nodded and watched him go, her heart full of some indefinable emotion that for no very good reason made her want to cry.

On Monday she popped up to the paediatric surgical ward before clinic to see William. He was doing well, still on tiny amounts of fluids only but his drip was down and he looked brighter even than he had on Friday.

She exchanged a few words with Mrs Griffin, who was full of praise for both Andrew and the surgeon, Ross Hamilton.

'I'm just so relieved — you have no idea how worried I've been!' she confided in Jennifer.

'Oh, I have,' Jennifer told her. 'I've got a son of seven, so I know just what agonies a mother goes through. Still, he's looking very good now — I'm sure it won't be long before he's driving you mad again!'

They exchanged a laughing goodbye, and she headed for the door just as Andrew swung it open. They exchanged slightly stilted greetings, conscious of the milling crowd of nurses and patients all around them.

'I came up to see William — he's looking well.'

'Isn't he? Ross did a good job. Have you got Peter's clinic?'

She nodded. 'Yes, I must go, I don't want to hold up proceedings. I'll see you this afternoon.'

He lifted a hand in a wave, and she left him and made her way down to Children's Outpatients, her day already immeasurably improved for having seen him even so briefly.

He did that to people, though, she realised, because he was always pleased to see them, always had a ready smile and a sympathetic ear.

Even when he was exhausted, which he quite often was, she had never known him lose his temper or get short with anyone. Unlike Nick, who had always been crabby and irritable when he was tired. During his house year she had kept Tim out of his way whenever possible, so that Nick could rest. Now, she wondered if she had done the right thing, because in the end he had accused her of avoiding him, and although she had denied it at the time later she had realised there might have been an element of truth in it. But then, if only Nick had been able to deal with his tiredness in the same way as Andrew, perhaps she wouldn't have grown to dread his return, and might have been a more willing wife. Who knows? she thought. Perhaps we might still have been together. And the old guilt came seeping back, drowning out her happiness.

* * *

It was another busy afternoon clinic, a special care baby unit follow-up with all the attendant crying and screaming and breast-feeding and consequent nappy-changing. While Jennifer ran backwards and forwards undressing and weighing and measuring and trying to orchestrate the timing so that the next patient was ready for Andrew before he needed to see them, he, of course, was in his element.

'Anybody would think you liked the smelly, leaky little things,' she teased, and he grinned.

'At least they aren't insubordinate! I mentioned a cup of tea hours ago.'

'Sorry, sir,' she laughed, and went and found Beattie, repeating his request.

When she took it in he was busy cooing at another baby, and she rolled her eyes and carried on with her weighing.

'I must get on,' he told her later as they cleared up after the last patient. 'I have to go back and feed Mummy-cat and make sure the kittens are all right, and I ought to check in SCBU before I go home.'

Jennifer laughed and shook her head. 'I don't know,' she murmured, 'between the babies and the kittens, you're just a pushover, aren't you?'

He shrugged her teasing off with a laugh. 'That's my life,' he said smilingly. 'Some of us are meant to nurture.'

'And you do it so beautifully. It's a shame you aren't married — all that pampering going to waste.'

'Are you volunteering?'

Her breath caught in her throat, and she stopped and looked up at him.

'Are you serious?'

He looked faintly surprised. 'Yes, I believe I am.'

She searched his craggy, lived-in face for an endless moment, then a slow smile curved her lips. She could do far worse than to hand herself over to this gentle man's attentions for the rest of her life. Warmth, comfort, security — it had a lot going for it, and she was sure in his gentle hands their lovemaking would be filled with tenderness, if not the passion of first love. Lord knows that can wane, she thought wryly. There was no mention of love, but at their age there were more important things, like Tim. And he would be a wonderful father, of that she was certain.

She looked up into his eyes. 'You're sure?'

He nodded slowly. 'Yes — oh, yes, I'm sure.'

'Then yes, I believe I am volunteering.'

'Perhaps you'd better think about it.'

She shook her head. 'No. There's nothing to think about.'

He opened his arms and she stepped into them and found herself wrapped hard against his massive chest.

'You won't regret it, I promise you,' he told her, his voice gruff with emotion. 'I'll do everything in my power to make you both happy.'

'You already have,' she told him, and, tipping back her head, she sealed the pact with a kiss.

CHAPTER THREE

TUESDAY was one of those chaotic days when children were sick in the clinic and babies screamed endlessly. Jennifer's staff nurse, Sarah Bright, was off sick and Peter Travers was coping without an SHO because Maggie Bradshaw, plagued by morning sickness, and given up work three months early and her replacement hadn't yet materialised.

She hadn't seen Andrew since the end of yesterday's clinic as his evening had already been totally committed. Now he was on the wards and she didn't see him until he popped down at lunchtime and cornered her in the kitchen snatching a cup of coffee.

'This place is like Piccadilly. I don't suppose you can get away?'

She laughed mirthlessly. 'Are you kidding? This is my first cup of coffee all morning.'

He glanced round and smiled. 'I suppose I am. Look, I know it's short notice, but could we make dinner tonight? I could bring a takeaway if you can't get a babysitter.'

Jennifer shook her head regretfully. 'No, sorry. Tim has Cubs and it's impossible to get him organised and fed and into bed at a decent hour. How about tomorrow?'

He shook his head. 'I'm giving a lecture — oh, damn. Thursday? No, I'm on call again.'

'The weekend?' she suggested hopefully. 'Tim is away with his father. . .'

Andrew closed his eyes and let out a harsh sigh. 'I've got to go to a conference. Next Monday?'

'You're on call again.'

'Oh, hell. This is ridiculous.'

She laughed softly. 'You'll forget what I look like soon.'

'No chance,' he said softly, and his voice held a wealth of warmth and emotion. 'Marry me soon, Jennifer. Then maybe between midnight and six in the morning we might get time to say hello when we aren't surrounded by people.'

She chuckled. 'Do you suppose we can find the time to do the deed?'

'We'll make time,' he growled softly. 'I must go, you've got work to do.' He leant over and brushed her lips with his, then, turning on his heel, he strode out through the department, exchanging greetings with the secretary on the way past.

She didn't see him again until the following day, at the paediatric diabetic clinic.

As usual they were rushed off their feet, but at least the load was shared by the dietician.

They had a new patient, a little boy of five who had been admitted in a diabetic coma four weeks previously. He had presented with a history of increased thirst, weight loss and listlessness which his mother had put down to the heat and nerves about returning to school, until the morning she found she couldn't rouse him. He had been stabilised and was now on insulin and coming back for his first check-up.

'How are you getting on with Paul's injections, Mrs Downing?' Andrew asked his mother.

'Oh, not so bad, I suppose. He doesn't like it very much, but I think we've got round it now. If he's a good boy, I give him a sweetie, don't I, darling?'

Paul nodded.

'Um — what sort of sweet, Mrs Downing?' Andrew asked her.

'Well, that depends what's around,' she said innocently. 'This morning it was a few squares of chocolate.'

'Ordinary chocolate?'

'Yes — well, we tried the diabetic chocolate but it gave him terrible diarrhoea.'

Andrew sighed. 'Mrs Downing, your son really mustn't have sweets, they're very bad for him. In order to keep him stable, he has to have sensible, high-fibre foods that will deliver the calories he needs gradually over a period of a few hours, not a sudden shock of sugar then nothing.'

'Oh, but I still give him the other food as well,' she assured him.

'And how's his blood-sugar level been?'

For the first time she looked vaguely uncomfortable. 'Oh, well, I suppose it's been all right.'

'Do you test it before every injection?'

She shifted awkwardly. 'No, not *every* injection. Well, he hates it so when I prick his little finger, but surely I can tell just by looking at him? I mean, he hasn't gone funny or anything. . .' She trailed off and flushed. 'Well, you try doing it when he's screaming blue murder and won't co-operate!'

Jennifer could see Andrew's frustration as he turned

to her. 'Sister, would you, please? We'll need bloods anyway for HbA1.'

'Of course. Paul, could you roll up your sleeve for me, darling, so I can put this strap on? That's lovely. Right, you hold this little bottle for me and see if you can turn it round and round while I just have a look at your arm here. Oh, that's lovely! You've got very clever veins, haven't you? What a good boy. Just a little tickle and it'll soon be over — well done. Keep the bottle turning — that's lovely. Good lad. All right, now,' she released the strap, laid a swab over the puncture and withdrew the needle. 'Could you hold that on there for me, nice and tight? Well done. There's a good boy.' She gave him a bright smile, ruffled his hair and winked.

While she waited for the result from the blood analyser, she bottled and labelled the blood for the lab, and disposed of the used syringe in the sharps bin, then put a plaster on Paul's arm.

'Well?'

She turned to Andrew and shook her head. 'Sky high. The urine was, too.'

She told him the result and he frowned. 'Mrs Downing, if you can't manage the finger prick each time, you must test his urine. It's not as accurate, of course, but it's better than nothing, and if you find it's high, then you must test his blood as well. Do you understand? Especially in the early stages until he's stable. If you can't manage that, I'm afraid we'll have to have him in and do it for you here, and we don't want to do that, but you really must understand that high blood sugar can lead to all sorts of problems for Paul later in life, like heart disease, kidney problems, eye trouble — sometimes we just have to be cruel to be kind, and the last thing you must do is bribe him with sweets.'

'Well, what would you suggest?' she asked defensively.

'You could perhaps offer him a treat — a day out at the weekend if he's been good about his diet and treatment, taking him to the cinema or the zoo, buying him something he particularly wants, but don't let him hold you to ransom. It's a part of his life from now on, and if you're firm he'll very quickly grow used to it and accept it. If he feels he can wind you round his little finger, he'll do it. They're great psychologists.'

He jotted down something in the notes, and handed them to Jennifer. 'Could you take Mrs Downing and Paul through to the dietician please, Sister? And I'll see you again in two weeks, Mrs Downing, to see how you're getting on.'

'Thank you, Dr Barrett,' she replied, somewhat stiffly. She was obviously chastened and didn't like the feel of it.

Jennifer schooled her expression, and held out her hand to Paul. 'Come on then, Paul,' she said with a smile, and he put down the aeroplane he was playing with and slipped his hand into hers. 'Let's go and talk about what you can have to eat, shall we?'

She delivered them to the dietician's waiting area and popped her head round the door, quickly filling her in on the problem.

She rolled her eyes. 'Silly woman. OK, I'll see her now. Thanks.'

Jennifer showed them in and went back into Andrew's office.

'Coffee?'

He sighed. 'No, not yet. I'll see the next one first, otherwise I'll never get done. God, what a stupid woman! Fancy bribing a diabetic with chocolate!'

'I can see her point ——'

'So can I, but nevertheless, you'd think she'd have the common sense ——'

Jennifer smiled. 'You're doing it again, you know. Assuming that the average parent has the intelligence to override maternal instinct. It isn't always easy.'

He sighed again, and returned her smile. 'I know. You've managed, though. I imagine it would have been easy to spoil him after your divorce, but Tim's a credit to you. He's a delightful child.'

She flushed slightly, unreasonably pleased by his words. 'Thank you.'

'My pleasure. Come here, I haven't kissed you for days.'

There was a tap on the door and Janet stuck her head round. 'Just had A and E on the phone — Suzanne Hooper, one of ours, admitted from school on the verge of a hypo. They've brought her round with Lucozade and biscuits. Can we fit her in? Mr Lawrence thinks she's abusing her diet — anorexia or bulimia.'

He groaned. 'Oh, no. Have we got the notes up here?'

'Uh-huh.' She waggled them at him. 'Shall I tell them you'll see her in the clinic?'

'Yes, why not? It'll save time if I don't have to go down there. Ask them to keep her there for now, resting, and we'll see her at the end. Try and get hold of her mother, too, if they haven't done it yet.'

'OK.'

The door closed.

'Now, where were we?' he murmured.

She gave a rueful laugh. 'Halfway through a busy clinic.'

He closed his eyes and sighed theatrically. 'Story of my life.' His eyes opened, and he grinned. 'Maybe later?'

'Maybe.'

She smiled and went out into the corridor. 'Stephen Clarke, please.'

Andrew agreed with Jack Lawrence's diagnosis on Suzanne Hooper. She was visibly thinner, much thinner than she should have been, and according to her mother was eating well.

'Sometimes I think she eats too much, but she never seems to go over, only under. I can't understand it.'

Andrew glanced at the notes. 'When were you due to see me again?'

'In two weeks. I was going to say something then, because it didn't seem too drastic and I didn't want to worry her, but I'm so glad we've seen you today.'

He nodded. 'OK, well, look, I'd like Sister Davidson to take Suzanne and run all the usual tests on her — blood, urine, height, weight and so on, and perhaps you could answer a few questions, then I'll have a chat to her on her own in a minute and see if there's anything we can find out to help sort her out. OK?'

A few minutes later Jennifer showed Mrs Hooper out and took the results and Suzanne back in to Andrew.

'Her blood sugar is still a little low, but her weight's

down four kilos since her last visit and she's grown nearly a centimetre.'

He nodded, swivelled round in his chair, stretched his legs out and gave the girl a level look. 'Why are you doing it?'

She blinked innocently. 'Doing what? I eat all the right things ——'

'And then make yourself sick. Why? You aren't overweight — in fact, you're under the third centile for your age and height. That means you are in the lightest three per cent of your population group. Do you understand?'

She nodded. 'I still don't see what makes you think I'm doing that.'

He shrugged. 'The weight loss, the fact that you're seen to be eating, your constant hypos — the faint, lingering smell of vomit on your clothes?'

She swallowed and looked away.

'Suzanne, we want to help you, but we can't if you won't talk to us.'

'You won't understand,' she said flatly. 'Nobody understands.'

'Try me.'

Eventually she shrugged. 'Nobody eats anything at school — they all pick at things, and they're all dead skinny, but I have to have all this food and I'm huge!'

Andrew's brows quirked. 'Huge?'

'I'm ugly,' she whispered. 'All fat and horrible — you should see my friends. They hardly eat a thing, and I have to sit down and gorge my way through great piles of food and get fatter and fatter ——'

She broke off and swallowed hard, obviously revolted by the thought of eating.

Andrew shook his head slowly. 'Suzanne, listen to me. Your body needs food. Your friends are being very foolish, and after a while they'll become ill. What you don't see and what they won't dare to admit is that they probably all eat secretly at home — a Mars bar on the bus, a sandwich in the middle of the night when they think no one's looking. But because of your diabetes you can't afford to abuse your system like that —'

'No!' she shouted. 'Because of my bloody diabetes I have to be different — well, I won't be different, and if I have to be different, then I'll kill myself!'

He shrugged. 'You're doing that at the moment,' he told her calmly. 'Carry on like this and it won't be long. And all your friends will grow up and get married and have babies and do interesting things with their lives, see interesting places, meet all sorts of fascinating people, and you'll just be a memory.'

She hunched her shoulders. 'So?'

'Well, don't you think that's rather a waste? There's nothing you couldn't do, you know, provided you're sensible. If you want to stay slim, we can maintain your diet at a level which will permit that. Provided all your intake is of foods which are of high nutritional value, you'll remain perfectly healthy, but you can't get away with eating junk food. Now, why don't we see if we can work out a better way of keeping you with us? Because I don't think you really want to die, do you?'

Her shoulders trembled, and then suddenly a great sob was wrenched from her chest.

'I want my mum,' she hiccuped, and Andrew patted her shoulder and stood up.

'I'll get her.'

She was there in a second, arms round her daughter, comforting her worldlessly while Andrew explained what had been going on.

Eventually they left, having seen the dietician and with their appointment for a fortnight left in place.

Andrew glanced wearily at his watch and sighed.

'No lunch again, I'm late for my ward round. And I lecture them about nutrition!'

Jennifer shook her head. 'Go past the canteen and grab a sandwich and eat it on the way. There's too much of you to live on love and fresh air.'

He laughed. 'Chance'd be a fine thing, bottled up in here without so much as a kiss to keep me going.'

He hugged her against him and brushed his lips over hers, pulling himself away reluctantly. 'Don't start me off, there isn't time,' he told her wryly.

'There's never time,' she sighed.

'No—but there will be. What are you doing on the tenth of October?'

She laughed. 'I don't know. Why don't you tell me?'

He grinned. 'It's the Barringtons' official send-off before they sail the Atlantic. It's not really my sort of thing, but Michael's done a lot for disabled children, including this jaunt, and I just feel I'd like to support him. Anyway, it's an opportunity to see you.'

'Hardly alone, though?'

He hugged her. 'There's always later. Hang in there.' He kissed her again lightly, winked and made a great production of dragging himself away. With a rueful smile she watched him go. Would there ever be time for them? They hadn't even had time to buy a ring— although they probably wouldn't bother. It was hardly a romantic match, after all.

She sighed again and set about clearing up the department ready for the next clinic.

It was as chaotic at the cystic fibrosis clinic on Thursday afternoon, but Friday was quieter for a change and he was able to get away at four for his conference in London.

She was glad to get away early, too, because Tim was spending the weekend with his father and she had to finish getting his things ready to take.

She saw them off at six, and then spent the weekend doing all the things she should have done the previous weekend instead of being pampered, and trying not to worry about Tim's solemn face and lack of enthusiasm about seeing his father.

It was a relief when the doorbell rang on Sunday evening, a little earlier than usual. She opened the door and gave Tim a hug, then looked up into her ex-husband's startling cornflower-blue eyes. 'Hi. How's it been?'

He returned her look levelly. 'Interesting. Mind if I come in? I've got something to tell you.'

She opened the door. 'I've got something to tell you, too. Would you like a drink?'

'Coffee will do fine. I'm driving.'

'That never used to worry you.'

He gave a short laugh. 'People change, Jen.'

Privately she doubted it, but said nothing. She showed him into the little sitting-room and left him there while she put the kettle on. When she went back he was standing at the window, looking out at the darkening sky. Funny, she had always thought he was tall, but compared to Andrew he seemed much shorter than before, which was ridiculous because she knew he was over six foot. His face was finely chiselled, conventionally handsome, his lips full and sensuous, but set now in an uncompromising line. He turned towards her, jiggling his change.

'So, who's Andrew?' he asked deceptively casually.

Oh, lord, whatever had Tim said? 'Er — one of the paediatric consultants.'

'Tim's been talking about him all weekend. He's obviously quite an influence.'

She wondered quite where to start, but Nick didn't give her time to worry.

'Look, on the subject of influence, I've been thinking about Tim. I know over the years I've not taken very much interest in him, and God knows we don't get on all that well when we are together, but I've decided it's time to change all that.'

'And how do you plan to set about this dramatic change?' she asked lightly.

'Easy. I want to see more of him — and you.' He stepped towards her and brushed her cheek with his knuckles, his eyes sweeping over her possessively. 'You're lovely, Jen, beautiful as ever. I miss you. I think maybe I was hasty walking out on you four years ago. Anyway, fate's handed me a second chance. One of your orthopaedic SRs is taking a sabbatical for two months, and I've got until January before I start my next job, so I applied. I start at the beginning of October.'

She was stunned. That was only little more than a week away, and he would be back in her life, apparently seeking to take up where they had left off. . .

'Nick, what exactly are you saying?'

His hands cupped her shoulders, and his eyes burned

with sincerity. 'That I think leaving you was a mistake. I should have stayed, toughed it out and worked on our relationship, but I was too tired and busy and immature. I've changed, Jen. I want another chance.'

He drew her towards him, but as she felt the brush of his lips she turned aside.

'No. Nick, listen, I have to talk to you. It's about Andrew.'

'Your pet paediatrician? What about him?'

'I — we spent last weekend with him.'

'I gathered that.' His voice was icy. 'Did you sleep with him?'

She drew in a shocked breath. 'No — not that it's any business of yours, but no, I didn't and I haven't.' She shot him a keen look, a sudden and unpleasant idea entering her head. 'Is that what this is all about? These sudden second thoughts of yours? Don't tell me you're jealous?'

He laughed shortly. 'Of course not — it's rather late for that, don't you think? Anyway, I knew about the job long before I heard about Andrew. No, it's just that it would be rather inconvenient if you were in the middle of a heavy relationship, but you're clearly not, so that's all right, then.'

'Not exactly.' She hesitated a second, then carried on, 'He asked me to marry him. I said yes.'

Nick stepped back and turned away, thrusting his hands into his pockets and jiggling his change. It was something he always did when he was playing for time. After a moment he turned back to her, his smile strained. 'Well, it looks as if I've come back just in the nick of time then, doesn't it?'

* * *

It was an awful week. Apart from fleeting glimpses and lightning phone calls she didn't see Andrew at all until the cystic fibrosis clinic on Thursday afternoon. Nick, however, phoned almost daily. To give him his due he was persistent, but then he always had wanted things that were slightly out of reach.

Andrew was late, held up by an emergency admission. She dropped a stack of notes on the desk and started without him, doing weights and heights and lung-volume tests. One little boy, Anthony Craven, had to have repeat X-rays to see if the infiltrates, or plugs of mucus, seen in his last X-ray had cleared up following appropriate antibiotics treatment.

She sent him off with his parents to the X-ray department, and then Andrew appeared and called her into his office, closing the door behind her.

'I've missed you,' he said softly.

She wanted to walk into his arms and lay her head on his shoulder and tell him to make it better, but she couldn't, it wasn't fair. Instead she took a step backwards and twisted her fingers together.

'Can you come round tonight? I know you're on call, but — '

'I'm not on call — I'm on for the weekend so Peter's doing tonight. I've got a child in ITU I might have to go and see, but I should be free for most of the evening. Why?'

She shrugged helplessly. 'I have to talk to you. Andrew, there's something we need to discuss, and it really can't wait.'

He looked at her keenly. 'Are you having second thoughts?'

'Yes — no — not exactly. Look, I can't explain here.

Can you come round tonight? After eight? I need to get Tim to bed first.'

He nodded. 'OK.' He drew a deep breath and let it out slowly. 'I suppose we ought to start the clinic. Who's first?'

The clinic proceeded normally, their behaviour quite unremarkable. No one seeing them would have realised the turmoil inside either of them. Jennifer was her usual friendly, open self, and Andrew was as calm and placid as ever, quietly competent, listening and percussing and examining X-ray plates, pointing out to parents the areas of concern, involving them in their children's treatment.

Anthony Craven, the seven-year-old who had been sent to X-Ray, came back with a set of plates that showed the infiltrates in the upper lobes of his right lung had failed to clear up with treatment.

'Right,' Andrew told her parents. 'I think what that means is that he's got a thing called allergic bronchopulmonary aspergillosis — in other words, a fungal infection. That's borne out by the brown plugs in his sputum and the raised level of immunoglobulin E in his blood, as well as the wheezy cough. Now, we have to treat this with an oral steroid called prednisolone, and that will get rid of the irritating cough and clear up the mess in his lungs. He'll need to take it until he's better, and then for a month after that to ensure he stays better.' He scribbled the prescription and handed it to them. 'The hospital dispensary will give you that, and I'd better see Anthony again in four weeks. OK? In the meantime, keep a look out for any deterioration that could be due to another infection, because this isn't an antibiotic and it may supress his ability to deal with infection caused by bacteria.'

He watched them leave, then glanced up at Jennifer. 'Who's next?'

'That's it. The Longs didn't show.'

He frowned. 'What? Jackie had a pseudomonas infection that I wanted to follow up. Damn, why are parents so irresponsible?'

'Maybe they felt she was better. I think they find the travel cost quite a burden — he's on invalidity benefit after an agricultural accident, and they live out in the sticks. Perhaps they just can't afford to get here.'

His frown deepened. 'But they're entitled to help with travel —'

'Perhaps they don't like to take it? They have their pride, Andrew.'

'And it competes with their daughter's health?'

Jennifer lifted her shoulders. 'Maybe she seemed better.'

He sighed. 'Maybe. I still want to see her. I'll get Janet to write and make them another appointment, and I'll ring the GP, just in case there's been a problem we don't know about.' He glanced at his watch, then stood up, shrugging on his jacket. 'Right, I'll go and have a look at my patients just to pre-empt any crises, and I'll see you at eight.'

She nodded unhappily. 'OK. Thanks.'

He tipped her chin with his finger and made her meet his eyes. They were warm and gentle and full of concern. 'Whatever it is, we can work it out,' he promised. Then he brushed her lips with his and left her.

She closed her eyes. 'Oh, Andrew, if only it were that simple. . .'

The doorbell rang at eight precisely, and Jennifer let him in, her heart leaden. She was enormously relieved that he hadn't brought her flowers or chocolates or some other trinket.

'Can I get you a drink? Tea or coffee or something?' she asked tensely.

'Coffee, please. The child in ITU is sliding downhill, and I have a feeling it's going to be a long night.'

'Oh. Right.' She went into the kitchen and filled the kettle, then plugged it in and stood like a zombie, staring out of the window. She saw him come in and stand behind her, meeting her eyes in the window. His hands came up and cupped her shoulders, and she felt the solid warmth of his body behind her. Oddly, it gave her the strength to talk to him.

'I've got a problem,' she told him at last.

His smile was wry but gentle. 'I gathered that. Why don't you tell me about it?'

She drew a deep breath. 'It's Nick — my ex-husband. You know Clare and Michael Barrington are sailing the Atlantic? Nick's taking Michael's post for two months while he's away. He says he wants to see more of me and Tim, and he thinks he made a mistake.' She closed her eyes and swallowed. 'He wants another chance.'

He felt as if he had been hit by a tank. Credit where it's due, he thought aimlessly, staring at his reflection in the window, his face didn't betray his feelings by so much as a flicker.

'How do you feel about that?' he asked, and commended himself again on the even tenor of his voice.

Her shoulders lifted under his hands in a little shrug. 'I don't know. We had such a crazy relationship — first of all the wild parties and student squalor in the flat we shared, then me stuck at home with Tim while Nick worked sometimes a hundred and twenty hours a week in his house job — it was never a normal life. We didn't stand a chance, really.'

He dragged in a much needed breath. 'And you think you do now?'

Her shoulders lifted again. 'I don't know. We must stand more chance, I suppose.'

'Do you love him?'

He thought his heart was going to stop as he waited for her answer.

'I'm not sure. I did, once, but he hurt me very badly when he left. I don't know how I feel now.'

'And does he love you?'

'He says so.'

His hands tensed on her shoulders, and with an effort he relaxed them and squeezed gently. The last thing he wanted was to hurt her — just grab her and drag her off to his lair and defend her honour, he thought with a sick attempt at humour. He almost laughed aloud. His designs on her honour didn't extend to defence of it, he was honest enough to admit that, but in any case, defend it against whom, pray? Against her husband, the father of her child? It was Nick who should have been defending her honour, claiming her favours. He felt suddenly cold and sick at the thought, and his hands dropped to his sides.

'So what do you want to do now?' he asked bleakly.

Her shoulders lifted in a helpless shrug, and she met his eyes, her own huge and liquid in the glass.

The kettle boiled, blurring their reflections, and she turned away with a sigh and reached for two mugs.

'How does Tim feel?'

'He doesn't know. I don't know how he'll take it. I'm not sure how he feels about his father at all. He's very reserved with him. That's one of the areas Nick wants to try and improve. Tim knows he's coming to work here, but nothing else.'

She turned towards him at last, and he saw the lines of strain etched clearly on her face. He reached out and touched them with a blunt fingertip.

'Does Nick know about us?'

She nodded. 'Sort of. I told him you'd asked me to marry you.'

'And?'

'He said he'd come back in the nick of time.'

He sighed. 'Which is my coffee?'

'Either.'

He picked one up and went through into the sitting-room, lowering himself numbly on to the settee. She came and sat beside him, close enough for him to feel her warmth and the tremors that shook her.

'So what happens now? What do you want to do about us?'

She lowered her head and her hair fell round her face, screening it from sight. 'I don't know,' she said in a small voice. 'It seems so unfair to you, but he is Tim's father and I loved him once. Maybe I could again. I just don't know how I feel any more. I haven't given it any thought because he's been so difficult in the past I was just glad to be free, but now, if he really has

changed like he says, perhaps — who knows? Maybe it
could work. But I said I'd marry you and it's all so
complicated now, and I don't know what to do for the
best. . .'

She trailed off miserably, and he set his coffee down
and pulled her back into his arms. 'Jennifer, listen to
me. You must do whatever you feel is right, for you
and for Tim.'

'But I don't know what's right —— '

'So take the time to find out. You aren't sure how
you feel, and, as you say, it is complicated. So take me
out of the equation for now, and give Nick his chance,
if that's what you feel you want to do. Lay the ghost.
If you don't, you'll never be free to move on with your
life.'

'But what about you? It's so unfair to you, just
when. . .'

He gave her a little squeeze. 'Don't you worry about
me. I'll still be here, no matter what you decide. You
can always talk to me, Jennifer. I'm always around. If
you need a friend, I'm here.'

'Oh, Andrew, I couldn't, that's so cruel.'

He secretly agreed, but said nothing. What was there
to say? Apart from screaming 'What about me?', and
that just didn't seem terribly appropriate.

'Tim keeps saying he wants to go to your cottage and
see the kittens again, and I keep putting him off, but I
don't know how I can make him understand —— '

And then the storm broke, and he wrapped his arms
around her and cradled her gently while the cold
loneliness of reality sank into his shocked mind.

How could he compete with a man who had lived
with her for years, who knew her little ways and could

anticipate them? And if she wanted to be pampered? Nick would know exactly how to do it, and let's face it, he thought tiredly, he held all the cards. Tim was the centre of her life, and Nick was his father. When all was said and done, he was what Tim needed, and if Nick and Jennifer really stood a chance to rebuild their marriage, what kind of a man would stand in their way?

He smoothed back the hair from her damp face and pressed his lips against it, then eased away from her and stood up. She was quiet now, but he didn't feel he could hold his own emotions in check very much longer.

'I must go.'

She lifted her tearstained face and searched his eyes. 'Are you OK?'

He forced a smile, but the words wouldn't come. He nodded.

Jennifer got to her feet and walked to the door, reaching for the handle.

'Thank you for listening. I'm so sorry. . .'

It was only a hug, just a simple, honest-to-goodness hug of comfort — or, at least, that was what he'd intended. He rested his brow against hers and fought the urge to kiss her until all thoughts of her ex-husband were driven from her mind, but somehow he couldn't manage to release her — not yet, not until he had tasted her one more time. . .

'One last thing,' he said gruffly, unable to leave just yet, and, cupping her head in his hands, he bent his head and lowered his mouth to hers.

His kiss was quick and hard and savagely controlled, nothing deep or lingering or erotic in the brief touch of his lips on hers, but she must have sensed the roiling emotions that churned in his chest, and although he knew he hadn't hurt her, he sensed her fear.

She whimpered against his mouth, and he released her immediately, yanked open the door and strode quickly down the hall. He couldn't wait for the lift, but instead ran three at a time down the stairs and out to the car park.

Sitting in the car with the window open, he dragged in great chunks of air while he waited for his vision to clear. He wouldn't think about her in Nick's arms. He couldn't, or he'd go insane. She had been so nearly his that Saturday night. Why he stopped? Perhaps then he could have competed with this unknown adversary on more even ground.

And perhaps not. They had been married for years. Her body held no secrets for Nick; he would know just what to do to please her, whereas he, Andrew, out of practice and unfamiliar with her needs, would probably have made a disastrous mess of the whole event.

He folded his arms on the steering-wheel and dropped his head down, fighting the despair that rose up to swamp him. He had been so close to happiness this time. It had taken him years, and several false starts, but this time he really felt he had found what he was looking for, and he knew instinctively that he would never try again. If he lost Jennifer to Nick, he would never marry now, never have the son to sleep in his old bed, nor the daughter to walk down the aisle on his arm in years to come.

He would be alone for the rest of his life, filling the emptiness with work and more work, devoting himself by day to the children in his care and rattling round an empty house all evening with just the cats for company.

If Nick won.

He lifted his head. Perhaps he still stood a chance, but it would be a passive fight, one he would have to stand back and watch. One thing was sure, the suspense would be agony.

His bleep squawked in the silence, and he stared at it as if he had never seen it before. Gradually his mind cleared, and after a second he started the engine and pulled slowly away.

CHAPTER FOUR

JENNIFER eyed Andrew worriedly the next day. His eyes were red-rimmed, and he looked exhausted, as if he hadn't slept all night.

'Are you OK?' she asked, concerned.

His smile was a little strained. 'One of those nights. What have we got this afternoon?'

'The usual mixed bag. The first one is a little girl called Gemma Edwards, aged four and a half, recurrent UTIs. GP thinks it might be reflux.'

'OK, we'll have a look at her, run a few tests on her urine and perhaps do a micturating cystourethrogram and renal ultrasound. Is she on antibiotics at the moment?'

She scanned the notes and shook her head. 'Not according to this.'

'Right, let's see her. And Jennifer?'

She turned back at the door.

'I meant what I said. If you need someone to talk to, I'm here.'

She felt her lip wobble, and then firmed it. 'Thanks.' She went out into the waiting-room and called Mrs Edwards and Gemma, and watched as the little girl bounced towards her, smiling.

'Hello, Gemma,' she greeted her, and smiled at the mother. 'Come on in. This is Dr Barrett.'

He stood up and shook her hand, then seated them.

'Right, Mrs Edwards, I gather Gemma's been having a lot of urinary infections. When did it start?'

While the mother filled them in on the background history, Andrew looked in Gemma's eyes, ears, throat and checked the inside of her eyelids to see if she was anaemic.

'OK, poppet, let's slip your things off and have a look at your tummy, could we?'

She obligingly struggled out of her tracksuit and Jennifer helped her climb on to the couch. Andrew examined her carefully and thoroughly, talking to her all the time to reassure her. Then he straightened up and winked. 'Good girl. Well, that looks fine. Have we got a urine sample?' he asked Jennifer, and she nodded.

'Yes, you've done a lovely wee for me, haven't you, darling?'

Gemma grinned and nodded.

'OK, we'll have bloods as well, I think, and a swab from the urethra. Can you book her in for a micturating cystourethrogram early next week? And we'll do the ultrasound at the same time.'

While Jennifer took the swab and some blood and then helped Gemma on with her clothes, Andrew washed his hands and sat down again with the mother.

'Right, Mrs Edwards, I want to run a couple of tests on Gemma to see if we can find out what's going wrong and why. One of the things I'll want to do is an X-ray type examination while she passes urine. Now, to do this we slip a little tube up into the bladder, fill it carefully with radio-opaque fluid and then we take the tube out and let her empty her bladder lying on the X-ray table in a sort of paddling pool. That way we can see if any of the fluid runs back towards the kidneys, which would indicate tricky valves in the bladder, possibly due to the recurrent infections, or maybe even causing them.

'Depending on what exactly we do find, we can then work out a course of action to prevent the infections recurring, but she must be careful not to wait too long before going and so building up too much pressure, because that tends to be when it happens and in the long run it can affect the kidneys.

'Now, in the meantime give her plenty to drink, not too strong, and make sure she empties her bladder very regularly. Get her up at night when you go to bed, and again first thing in the morning, and make sure you always wipe her bottom from the front to the back. It might be worth washing her every time she uses the loo, and try showering rather than sitting her in the bath.' His mouth tilted in a wry grin. 'I know it all sounds a bit like witchcraft, but very often it's all that's needed.'

Mrs Edwards smiled. 'It makes perfect sense to me. I used to have cystitis a lot when I first got married, and I tried all sorts of things.'

'And what worked?'

She flushed and laughed. 'All of them together, plus a little restraint in our—er——' she shot Gemma a look, and laughed again '—let's say nocturnal activities.'

Andrew grinned. 'Well, I don't think that's Gemma's problem, but it's quite possible that you've passed on a susceptibility to infection—perhaps slightly defective valves, or something minor like that. The investigations will reveal anything of that nature, and we can go from there. If you could bring her back next week, Sister Davidson will give you an appointment and we'll see what we can find out. OK?'

He stood up and showed them out, and after she had made the appointments Jennifer went back in.

'Lovely child. I don't suppose there's any possibility it is abuse?'

He didn't look surprised, Jennifer thought sadly. It was a sign of the times that such a thing could be considered almost routinely, although never without that awful sense of outrage.

Andrew considered her words and shook his head. 'I'm almost certain not. She's too happy and open, and there was no sign of any damage or bruising, or scarring, or anything which made me in the slightest bit suspicious. Why?'

Jennifer shrugged. 'It was just what the mother said about herself. Why did you check for bruising?'

He gave a wry and slightly bitter smile. 'Routine, isn't it? Has to be. What a sick society we live in. As for the mother, I think her history is probably totally unconnected. Still, we'll watch the child. What's next?'

And so the day progressed, an endless stream of children, some too large, some too small, some with tummy-ache for no good reason, some with nothing apparently wrong but simply failing to thrive, and through it all Jennifer watched Andrew at work and marvelled at his skill and gentleness, the way he sorted out the grain from the chaff of parental ramblings about the symptoms until he could produce a picture clear enough to work with.

He never patronised, she realised, never talked down even to the most ignorant of parents, but always managed to couch instructions and explanations in language appropriate to their level of understanding.

In short, he was an intuitive and gifted physican, and she knew she was very fortunate to have the opportunity to work with him.

By the end of the day he looked more tired than ever, and she took him a cup of tea and stood warily watching him as he gulped it down.

'You look awful,' she said quietly, and he set the cup down and shot her a wry smile.

'You don't say, after that clinic!' He picked up his jacket and shrugged it on.

'How's your child in ITU?' she asked, desperate for some reason not to let him go just yet. A second later she wished she had, as his face grew grave.

'Grim. Severe head injuries. The parents refuse to let us turn off the life-support machine, even though there's no hope. The brain-stem tests show no activity at all, but they can't come to terms with it.'

'I can see why,' she said quietly. 'If it was Tim. . .'

'I can see why, too. That's why I sat with them all night, and went up at lunchtime to talk to them again.'

'Any change?'

He shook his head and let out his breath on a short sigh. 'No. No change. I'd better go and feed the cats and cut the grass while the going's good. I'm on call and you can be sure I'll be in all weekend.'

He looked at her thoughtfully. 'Are you doing anything tomorrow?'

She laughed mirthlessly, thinking of the dismal little flat that resiliently defied her attempts at homemaking. 'The usual.'

'Would you and Tim like to come over and see the

kittens? I'll have to come in in the morning, so I could pick you up on my way back and drop you home later.'

She hesitated, and he tipped her chin up and made her meet his eyes. They were gentle, as always, and as honest as the day is long. 'No strings, Jennifer. I just thought Tim would enjoy it, and it might take your mind off things.'

She almost laughed. How would being with him take her mind off the fact that she would lose him if she went back to Nick? But for Tim's sake she agreed, with reservations.

'Please, don't take this the wrong way, but I don't want him hurt. If I go back to Nick — I just don't want Tim to grow too dependent on you.'

His face hardened, and he dropped his hand. 'Do you really think I would do that? Use Tim to get to you? I hope I have more integrity.'

'Andrew, I didn't mean — I didn't think for a moment you would use him, but he thinks so much of you, and if I go back to Nick we'll have to move back to London with him, and he'll never see you again.'

A fleeting pain crossed his face, and he turned away. 'Don't worry, Jennifer. I won't let him get too dependent on me.' Or vice versa, he could have added, but he bit his tongue.

'Golly, Mum, they're huge! Oh, look, they've got their eyes open — oh, Mum, can we have one when they're bigger? Please please please?'

'Oh, Tim.' She put her arm round his slight shoulders and hugged him tight. If Nick hadn't had a sudden fit of conscience, Tim could have had all the kittens. . . 'Darling, you know we can't in the flat.'

'So let's move!'

She looked up to Andrew for help. 'Tim, it isn't that simple. . . You can't just pack everything up and move. Where would we go? The flat's so handy for the hospital and your school, and all your friends are near——'

'We could live in the country. You love it, Mum, you said so. You even asked me if I would like to live in the country one day, so I know you want to. Go on, Mum, please?'

Andrew crouched down beside them. 'Tim, do you trust your mother?'

He looked astonished. 'Of course I do.'

'Well, then, don't you think you should trust her to do the best for you? I'm sure she's thought very hard about where you should live, and for now the flat is the right place. When it isn't the right place any more, then I'm sure you can trust her to choose a better place for you.'

'In the country?'

Andrew met her eyes and quirked a brow. 'Not necessarily. It might be somewhere quite different. The thing is, she'll do the best for you, and you'll have to trust her to know what the best is.'

His face was crestfallen. 'I suppose,' he mumbled, and looked back at the kittens. 'How soon will they grow up?'

Andrew smiled and tousled his hair. 'Don't you worry, son, they'll still be kittens for a long time yet. Anyway, they can't leave their mother for ages, they're too small.'

Just then Blu-Tack limped over to the little group in the corner of the kitchen, swiped a rough tongue over the backs of the kittens and sat down next to them, washing himself.

'He likes them,' Tim said in amazement.

'Oh, yes.' Andrew smiled. 'He seems to have adopted them. He brings Mummy-cat mice and birds and all sorts of presents.'

Tim wrinkled his nose. 'Gross,' he mumbled.

Jennifer chuckled. 'It's just nature, darling.'

'I'm going to be a vegetarian like Andrew. Dad's into nature — he eats yucky steaks with blood running out. It's disgusting.'

Andrew laughed, and Jennifer gave him a funny look. 'Are you vegetarian?'

'Not really. I eat fish and chicken sometimes.'

'Do you know, I didn't even notice? We eat so little red meat these days I can't remember if I like it!'

'Well, I don't!' Tim said firmly, and made a very expressive, 'yuck' sort of noise.

Andrew suppressed a smile. 'Do you want to go outside? It's lovely and sunny.'

'Can I feed the hens?'

Andrew glanced at Jennifer for confirmation, then nodded. 'OK, but don't go out of the gate or into the woods, all right?'

He nodded and scrambled to his feet, heading for the door. Jennifer watched him go, her face sad.

'What is it?'

She sighed and shook her head. 'He's a different child here. Sunny, cheerful, energetic — he loves it here so much. I don't know how he'll cope if we go back to London.'

'My grandmother had a saying. "Don't buy trouble,

it'll find you soon enough". I should worry about going back to London if and when it happens.'

She sighed again. Getting to his feet, Andrew held a hand down to her and helped her up, releasing her immediately. As if he hadn't really meant to touch her, she thought sadly.

'Cup of tea?'

'That would be lovely.'

He put the kettle on and it was almost boiled when his bleep went off. 'Oh, damn,' he muttered, and went to the phone in the hall. A few moments later he came back. 'I have to go in. The parents of the boy in ITU seem to have changed their minds, but they want to talk to me about transplants and things before they go any further.'

'Maybe they'll feel his life hasn't been wasted if he lives on in others.'

'Maybe. Frankly I doubt if they'll be that philosophical. It looks like it could be a long job, though, so I'd better take you back or you could be stuck here for hours.'

'Oh, dear, what a shame,' she said wryly.

His eyes searched her face. 'Do you want to stay?'

She shook her head and let her breath out on a heavy sigh. 'No. It's better if we don't.'

He took them back to the flat, and during the afternoon Nick rang to say he would be coming up to the hospital the following day to discuss accommodation and would like to come for lunch and perhaps take them out during the afternoon. She agreed to lunch, said she would discuss the afternoon with Tim and hung up, her emotions in turmoil.

How would she really feel about having him back in

her life? She had loved him so desperately, but he had let her down in such a hurtful way that she was unsure if she could forgive him. Did she still love him anyway? He had hurt Tim, too, with his earlier indifference. No amount of change of heart at this stage would take that earlier hurt away, but it might prevent any further damage.

She wished he and Tim got on better. Perhaps what they needed was more exposure to each other. Starting tomorrow.

'Tim, Daddy's coming up tomorrow. He's going to have lunch with us and then we're going out together. That's something to look forward to, isn't it?'

'I s'pose so,' he said woodenly, and shut himself in his bedroom with a book and didn't come out for hours.

Lunch was less of a strain than she had feared. Nick arrived punctually for once, and actually complimented her on the chicken pie she had made. After they had washed up together—another first, she thought with irony—she managed to talk him out of a visit to the speedway stadium in favour of Tim's favourite activity, a walk through the park to see the water birds on the little island, and then squirrel-spotting in the arboretum.

'Strange child,' he said thoughtfully as they strolled under the trees.

'He's not strange, Nick, he's just not like you,' Jennifer corrected gently.

'Same difference. He's a bit of a cuckoo really, isn't he?'

She held on to her temper with difficulty. 'Actually, he's a lot like me when I was a child.'

'Yes, but you were a girl—sorry, sorry!' He threw his hands up and grinned, and once again he was the boy she had fallen in love with. Her heart did a silly flip-flop and she looked quickly away. Heavens, would it really be such an easy conquest? If she could still feel like this with him, then could she marry him again? And if she did, would he and Tim learn to understand each other? She was sure Nick loved his son. Tim's love was rather more difficult to gauge, but she was sure it would come given time and gentle understanding.

Could it really be so simple?

'Jen. . .?'

She stopped and turned towards him. His face was serious now, his eyes for once not dancing with mischief but blazing with intensity.

'Tell me there's a chance for us.'

Her mouth was opening when Tim came running back. 'Mum, come and see—there's one of those bracket funguses we found with Andrew, and it's bright orange—look, it's amazing!'

Andrew! Reality hit her like a bucket of cold water. No, it couldn't be so simple after all. It was more complicated than she could have believed possible, and it was getting worse every day.

'Jen?'

'Give me time, Nick,' she stalled.

'I'm not a patient man.'

She shot him a wry look. 'You never were.'

How different two men could be. Andrew had told her to take all the time she needed. Nick was already hassling her before he had even moved up here. Could it really work? Five minutes ago she had thought so. Now she was not so sure.

As the beginning of October loomed, so her fears grew. Andrew was strangely remote, not unfriendly, but guarded. Not unnaturally, she thought with sadness, considering what she had done to him.

Gemma Edwards came back on Tuesday morning for her investigations into the recurrent urinary infections she had been having, and the radiologist found a slight bulge in both ureters on ultrasound that indicated the likelihood of reflux — an indication that was proved valid by the micturating cystourethrogram. As Gemma emptied her bladder, so the radio-opaque fluid ran back up both ureters and into the cavity in the centre of her kidneys, causing back-pressure that was likely to give rise to extensive scarring of the delicate kidney tissues.

Andrew referred her to a urologist, confident that there was no question of her condition being caused in any way by abuse, and with the possibility of surgery ahead to correct the defective valves in the bladder.

He was gentle and patient with Gemma, who found the whole experience very distressing, and with her mother who was naturally upset both by Gemma's reaction and the results.

Jennifer, who was having trouble with Tim, marvelled at his patience and went home at the end of the day determined to try harder with her sullen and uncommunicative son.

She failed, dismally.

Tim had Cubs and was difficult to get to bed afterwards. He had the beginnings of a cold, and was grotty and awkward, testing her resolution to the utmost, until in the end she sent him to bed in a temper.

Minutes later she heard him crying, and, full of remorse, she went in to him. Eventually he confessed he was worried about his father's arrival at the end of the week. They sat and talked for ages, until she finally managed to coax him into bed by ten, and the next morning he was sluggish, full of cold and reluctant to go to school.

As a result she was late and found the diabetic clinic delayed because her staff nurse was off again.

Andrew was understanding, which somehow just made it worse, and by coffee time she just wanted to go into a dark hole and cry her eyes out.

He found her slumped in the sluice, staring sightlessly at her feet, and pushed a cup of coffee into her hand. 'Drink this and tell Uncle Andrew all about it.'

She sighed and gulped the coffee, slopping it on her dress and swearing uncharacteristically under her breath.

'Come on, come and sit down and talk about it.'

She trailed him back to his office and dropped heavily into the chair, blotting half-heartedly at the mark on her dresss.

'Well?'

'Tim is dreading his father's arrival.'

'And you?'

She laughed shortly. 'What do you think? It's going to be awful.'

'Awful?'

She shrugged. 'I don't know what his expectations are going to be. Maybe he thinks he can pick up where we left off, but I'm not the person he walked out on any more, and I hope for his sake that he's not the man who left me or we're doomed to failure from the start. Oh, hell, I don't even know if I want it to work!' She set the coffee down and stood up, ramming her hands into her pockets. She had always thought wringing your hands was very theatrical. Now she realised it was just because she'd never felt distracted enough to want do do it!

Andrew's hands were warm and hard on her shoulders, kneading the tension from her knotted muscles and making tears well in her eyes.

'What am I going to do?' she asked in a small voice.

'You're going to finish your coffee, go and get Paul Downing and we'll see if his mother's stopped bribing him with chocolate. Then you'll bring in the next patient — is it Suzanne Hooper? — and so on.' His hands squeezed, and then dropped. 'One minute, one hour, one day at a time. Be patient. It'll all resolve itself one way or another given time.'

She turned to face him. 'How can you be so philosophical?'

His smile was wry and didn't quite reach those melted chocolate eyes. 'Practice,' he said quietly, and turned away. 'Let's see Paul now, can we?'

Mrs Downing had, indeed, stopping bribing Paul with chocolate. 'He hated me for a good few days, but gradually he's come to accept it. I'm amazed. I thought he'd be awful, but he's been a good boy, haven't you, darling?'

'I'm going to the zoo at half-term,' Paul told them earnestly. 'And then at Christmas we might go to stay with Granny in Wales and have a holiday in a hotel on the way home, and then next summer Daddy said maybe we can go to Euro Disney.'

'That child,' Andrew said to Jennifer after the Downings had left, 'is going to be so spoilt he'll be revolting.'

She smiled. 'At least the blood sugar's down.'

Andrew laughed. 'I suppose we should be grateful for small mercies. We'll see how he's doing in a month, or if the parents have run out of ways to ruin him. Is Suzanne Hooper here?'

'Yes — she looks ghastly. Thin and ill and generally on the verge of a hypo. I've done the blood and urine tests, they were both low, and her weight's down another three hundred grams.'

He wrinkled his nose. 'Not much.'

'No, but her clothes are heavier this time, and I think it's probably deliberate.'

He sighed. 'Wheel her in, then. I think it might be time to call in the clinical psychologist if you're right.'

She was, and he did. Suzanne was referred immediately, and an appointment was made for her the following day. Her mother was torn between relief that something was at last being done and fear that that something was a psychiatric referral.

'What a coil,' Andrew said as they left. 'Why can't the child have just one problem, not two?'

'Somebody's law, isn't it?' Jennifer suggested, and Andrew's mouth lifted in a wry grin.

'Very likely. Oh, well, we'll see in a month how she's got on. Who's next?'

The clinic ground to a halt just too late for them to have lunch, and Andrew went off to the wards leaving Jennifer rushing round clearing up before Peter Travers came down for his clinic and the rush started all over again.

In a way it was good, because it gave her no time to think that Nick was driving up from London late on the following day, ready to start work on the Friday morning.

She was nervy and irritable the next day during the CF clinic, and when it was over Andrew shut his door and trapped her.

'Talk to me.'

'Nick's coming tonight,' she said without preamble. 'I don't know how I'm going to cope. He's going to push me, and it's going to be difficult.'

'Have you got time for a bite in the canteen? It might help you unravel.'

She smiled wanly at him. 'No. Thanks, but I have to collect Tim and he's got a cold and is foul and unreasonable at the moment, and the flat's a tip and Nick's bound to drop in as soon as he gets his stuff unpacked — maybe before, if he's hungry. Who knows?'

Her laugh sounded strained, even to her own ears, and she moved quickly to the door, needing to escape.

'Jennifer?'

His quiet voice stopped her.

'You can always ring me.'

She shot him a grateful little smile. 'Thanks. I'll see you tomorrow.'

She cleared up quickly, collected Tim from the childminder and went home, to find Nick slouched against the door looking boyishly handsome and raffish in jeans and trainers and a sloganned sweatshirt.

'What kept you?' he said with a lazy grin, and her

heart sank. The place was chaotic, Tim was tired and hungry and she really didn't need to see him now, but he was moving up there for them, and the least she could do was offer him hospitality.

She forced a smile. 'Sorry. Have you eaten?'

He grinned again. 'Lifesaver. Got any steak?'

'Yuck,' Tim mumbled, and she squeezed his hand warningly.

'No, but there are some turkey burgers.'

'Oh, hell, no — how about going out for a meal? We could check out the hospital canteen.'

'No, Tim isn't well. You could get a takeaway and bring it back.'

'Done — Chinese, Indian or Pizza Hut?'

He looked hopefully at Tim, who dropped his eyes to the floor.

'Can we have salad? I just want something cold,' he croaked.

'Get whatever you like,' she told Nick. 'Anything would beat cooking tonight, and I'll do something simple for Tim while you get it.'

He looked momentarily nonplussed. 'But I don't know where to go ——'

'So ask someone,' she snapped, and then relented. 'Try past the hospital and the first road on the left — there's a Chinese there that's quite reasonable.'

'Oh — right. OK. I'll see you in a bit.'

She let herself in and Tim flopped on the settee, looking terribly small and defenceless.

'Is he going to be hanging around here a lot?' he asked suddenly.

'Daddy?' She paused in the act of gathering up the ironing and looked at Tim. 'Well — I don't know about hanging around, but he has moved up here so that he can see more of us for a while ——'

'What's the point? He doesn't like me.'

She put the ironing down and sat on the settee next to Tim. 'Tim—darling, he loves you very much. He just doesn't know you very well, and that's what he wants to change.'

'But I don't want things to change. I was happy the way it was.'

'Were you? Every time you went out with him for the weekend you came back unhappy.'

He shot her a miserable look. 'Yeah, but it wasn't very often. Now he's going to be here all the time and we won't be able to go and see the kittens and they'll be grown up by the time he goes away again. Anyway, I like Andrew better.'

Jennifer closed her eyes. Sometimes children just cut through all the superfluous issues straight to the heart of the matter. 'Darling, Andrew doesn't enter into this,' she told him, not quite truthfully. 'I'm sure if you knew your father better you'd like him, too. He's a good man.'

'So why didn't you stay married?' Tim asked with maddening logic.

She looked away. 'People make mistakes. Perhaps us getting divorced was one of them.'

Tim sat bolt upright. 'Are you and Daddy going to get married?'

'I don't know. How would you feel?'

He stood up and marched over to his bedroom door. 'I think that would be the stupidest thing in the world, 'cos he drives you mad all the time, and anyway, he lives in London. You'd hate it.'

And with that he went into his room, closed the door and refused to come out.

When Nick returned with the Chinese takeaway she had cleared up the flat a little and taken Tim in a salad which he was huffily ignoring.

'Where's Tim?' Nick asked.

'Sulking. You're going to have to tread very carefully with him.'

'Oh, bloody hell.' He set the bag down on the worktop in the kitchen and propped one lean hip against the cupboards. 'And you?'

'What about me?'

'Do I have to tread very carefully with you, too?'

She drew a deep breath. Might as well get it all out into the open at once.

'Frankly, yes. Don't imagine we're going to pick where we left off four years ago, Nick. I've got no intention of falling into your arms, not to mention your bed, so if you're cherishing any illusions on that score you can forget it.'

He laid a hand on his heart in a gesture of deep sincerity.

'Me?' he said in mock amazement. 'Darling girl, you do me an injustice.'

She met his twinkling eyes and laughed.

'Somehow I don't think so. But I mean it, don't forget. No hanky-panky, OK?'

He sighed. 'I had it all worked out.'

'I don't doubt it,' she told him drily. 'Are we going to eat tonight? I didn't have time for lunch.'

'Sure.' He reached for the bag. 'I got you beef chow mein, OK?'

Oh, well, red meat wouldn't kill her just once. Frankly she was hungry enough to eat a horse.

'That's fine, thanks.'

Conversation was stilted, and after they had eaten Nick voluntarily disappeared to unpack and settle into his quarters at the hospital—leaving the washing-up this time. That new leaf didn't stay turned very long! she thought with a flicker of black humour.

'Busy day tomorrow,' he said, and she nodded.

'Thanks for the meal. I really didn't want to cook.'

'You're welcome. Do I get a kiss goodnight?'

'Nick——'

'OK, OK, just an idea,' he laughed, throwing his hands up in the air. 'See you tomorrow.'

Somehow she didn't doubt it.

CHAPTER FIVE

IN FACT the clinics the next day were hectic in the extreme, and Jennifer didn't have time to make it up to the canteen for a meal, the only place she thought it likely that she would see Nick. She wasn't altogether sorry about that, but by one-thirty she was dying of hunger and thirst and ready to drop.

However Andrew, either mind-reading or because he hadn't seen Peter all morning and realised they must be busy, brought her down a sandwich at the start of the afternoon clinic and asked how the day was going.

'It's going,' she said shortly, and bit ungraciously into the sandwich.

He hid a smile. 'Cup of tea?'

'Make it yourself, the kettle's hot,' she told him crossly.

He cleared his throat and grinned. 'I was offering you one, actually.'

She met his eyes and flushed apologetically, suddenly conscious of her ungracious behaviour. 'I'm sorry—it's been one of those awful days,' she said wearily.

'I gathered.' He flicked the switch on the kettle and reached for a mug and a tea-bag. 'Did Nick arrive safely?'

She frowned. Had she imagined it, or was there a tightness in his voice? It was hard to tell over the noise of the kettle, but somehow. . .

'Yes, thanks. He was there when we got home.'

85

'Oh.'

'Yes, oh. Tim was foul, Nick was hungry and I didn't want to talk to either of them!'

He chuckled softly and passed her a brimming mug of tea. 'Drink up and stop worrying. They'll shake down.'

'I hope so. Just at the moment I don't have time to worry about it. There are altogether too many men in my life for comfort.'

'We'll have to narrow the field then, won't we?'

Startled, she glanced up over the top of her mug and her eyes clashed with Nick's, dancing with wicked blue lights. He was slouching in the doorway behind Andrew, looking for all the world like an escapee from a TV hospital sitcom in green theatre pyjamas, mask dangling round his neck, J-cloth hat tipped at a rakish angle on his tousled dark hair. Still startled, she took a gulp of tea just as he winked.

The consequences were fairly predictable. She choked, slopped her tea and sank against the cupboards, coughing weakly.

'Well, that's a dramatic reaction. Should I be flattered?' Nick drawled softly.

She closed her eyes and coughed once more, then forced herself to look up.

Both men were looking at her, Nick expectantly, Andrew with gentle concern.

She took a deep breath and waved a hand vaguely between them. 'Nick, this is Andrew Barrett,' she croaked. 'Andrew, my ex-husband, Nick Davidson.'

Then she stood back and waited.

Andrew, ever the gentleman, extended his hand and Nick grasped it briefly, his eyes boldly assessing.

'So, you're the competition.'

Jennifer glared at Nick, but Andrew merely met his challenging stare for a second, then smiled.

'Since we're obviously dispensing with the social pleasantries, will you excuse me? I have a clinic to start.'

'Sure — any chance of a cup of tea, Jen? I'm parched. Talk about chucked in at the deep end!'

In grim silence, she handed him the mug of tea Andrew had made for her. He drained it and grinned.

'Great. You've saved my life.' He ducked his head in the direction Andrew had taken. 'Bit of a stuffed shirt, isn't he?'

She glared at him. 'We aren't all as flamboyant as you.'

'All right, no need to be so touchy!'

'I don't have time for this,' she muttered, and, excusing herself, she went to follow Andrew.

Nick's hand on her arm detained her. 'What are you doing tonight?'

She glanced pointedly at his hand. 'Working late, unless I'm allowed to get on.'

His hand remained on her arm. 'And afterwards?'

'I don't know. Nothing, probably. Tim wasn't very well this morning, so my first priority is to see how he is.'

'May I come round?'

'Does it matter what I say?'

Nick gave an exasperated sigh. 'Of course it matters, Jen, but we have a lot to talk about.'

She met his eyes steadily. 'Yes, you're right, we have. I think we need some ground rules. Come round at eight-thirty — and make sure you've eaten first! Now I must get on.'

'Do you want the rest of this sandwich?'

She glared at him again, and sighed shortly. 'Have it.'

'You're too good to me.'

'And ain't that the truth!' she muttered as she walked away.

So that was the ex-husband, Tim's father, the man who wanted Jennifer back.

Andrew stood at the open window of his consulting-room and dragged in some fresh air, consciously relaxing his fists.

Damn the man, how dared he pinch her cup of tea? Couldn't he see she had been on the run all day and was exhausted? Of course he would have done if he'd had any perception at all, but Andrew had the distinct feeling the man couldn't see beyond the end of his self-centred and perfectly aquiline nose.

With a harsh sigh, he turned from the window. What chance did he stand, really? Beside Nick he must seem a clumsy ox, overlarge, heavy — granted, there wasn't an ounce of fat on him, but he was seriously big, and his face lacked the sculptured perfection of the younger man's. And Nick had youth on his side. He must be a good five years younger than Andrew, and it showed. The man was built like a film star, his shoulders broad but not heavy, his hips lean, his eyes lazy and sensuous, straying over Jennifer's body as if he owned her — damn him! He had a cocky self-assurance and sexual self-confidence that Andrew knew he could never emulate in a million years. And, as if that weren't enough, he had another, more insidious weapon.

He was Tim's father.

It was hard to believe, looking at him. In fact, if he hadn't known Jennifer so well, Andrew would have been forced to think that Tim was the child of another man, so different were they, but there was no way Jennifer would have played around. In fact, unless he was mistaken, Nick was the only man she had ever slept with—and that gave the damn man a hell of an advantage.

There was nothing quite like the loyalty of a woman to her first lover, he thought bitterly.

He sighed again and threw himself into the big, sturdy chair in front of his desk. It groaned in protest, and he glared at it balefully. '*Et tu, Brute*?' he muttered, and then the door opened and Jennifer came in.

She shut the door behind her and leant on it, meeting his eyes, her chin tilted slightly as if she was expecting trouble. He could see she was uncomfortable, but with typical courage she was facing it head-on.

'I'm sorry about that.'

Andrew shrugged. 'That's OK. We had to meet sooner or later. It's just got it over with.'

She smiled a little warily. 'I've told him not to come down here again.'

'Jennifer, it really doesn't matter. Can we get on?'

'Oh—of course. Sorry. Here are the notes.'

She failed to concentrate—perhaps predictably, and for the first time Andrew grew short with her.

She apologised, her eyes like huge bruises in her face, and he felt a heel. It didn't improve his temper, and it finally snapped mid-afternoon.

He was seeing a new patient, a boy of ten, referred by his GP because the parents were at their wits' end with him.

'He used to be so enthusiastic about everything, and he was fine when we first moved up here from London two years ago, but for the last year he's been so difficult and awkward, and just recently we haven't been able to wake him, he won't do his homework, he's sullen and uncooperative and we've run out of ideas,' his mother said directly.

'Right, let's have a look at you.'

He gave the boy a thorough and rigorous physical, and then sat back down, facing Simon's mother. 'Mrs Dean, may I have a few moments alone with Simon?'

She looked surprised, but agreed readily enough.

'Sister, if you don't mind?' Andrew said pointedly to Jennifer, who was standing there looking vague.

She blinked, startled. 'Do you want me to go?'

'Alone, I said,' he told her tartly, and she recoiled as if he'd slapped her.

'Fine — excuse me.'

Andrew closed his eyes. Why had he spoken to her like that, today of all days? As if she didn't have enough problems without him bitching at her unnecessarily. He turned his attention to the boy.

He was sitting hunched in the chair, picking idly at the edge of the plastic seat. He looked sulky and recalcitrant, and somehow despairing.

Andrew leant back in his chair and steepled his fingers. 'OK, Simon, what's it all about?' he asked bluntly.

'I'm just tired.'

'Are you? Or are you bored?'

He sighed, and then met Andrew's eyes. 'I'm bored — the school's trash. I had a great time in London, the school was brilliant, but this one is really gross and the kids are so stupid — they muck about all the time and never get on with anything, and the work's so *boring*.'

'And yet you can't do it.'

'Of course I can do it!'

'So why don't you?'

'Can't be bothered. I can do it standing on my head, but what's the point? I'm not learning anything.'

Andrew pursed his lips and watched the boy for a moment. It had been a wild guess, but apparently an inspired one. 'Have you ever had an IQ test?' he asked.

He shook his head. 'No, don't think so. Standard assessment tests in school, but they don't call them IQ tests.'

Andrew flicked him a medical journal, open at a page on the misdiagnosis of cystic fibrosis. 'Read that out loud to me, could you?'

He stumbled a little on the long words, but his reading was fluent, rapid and expressive, and he managed to make sense of the content, too. After a moment he looked up. 'That's interesting. Do you treat children with CF here?'

Andrew nodded. 'Yes. Do you know anything about it?'

He shrugged. 'I had a friend in London with CF. I used to visit him in hospital sometimes. It was fascinating in a gruesome sort of way.'

'Does medicine interest you?'

'Oh, yes, I love it!' Hope flared in his eyes, as if for the first time someone was paying attention to the person he was, but then as quickly as it had appeared, the hope was extinguished. 'I'd like to do medical research, but it's no good talking to my parents, they just say the way I'm doing at school I'll be lucky not to get chucked out.'

Andrew laughed. 'I think they're probably right, but it's not because you're thick, is it?'

'I just wish there was something interesting to do.'

'Have you tried asking the staff?'

He shrugged. 'They won't give it to me. They say they don't want me getting ahead.'

'I think you are ahead, that's the trouble,' Andrew told him. 'And if that's the case, we ought to do something. Let me talk to your mother for a minute.'

'Alone?'

He grinned. 'Yes. We don't need your input for a moment, young man. Go and sit in the waiting-room and try not to be a nuisance.'

He managed to look wounded and yet mischievous at once, and Andrew laughed. 'Go on, out. Send your mother in, please.'

Mrs Dean was astonished at Andrew's diagnosis.

'That's it? He's too clever?'

'I believe so. There's nothing physically that either I or the GP can find wrong with him, and he read this aloud to me with very little less hesitation than I would have.'

He handed the journal to Mrs Dean, and her eyes widened. 'He read that?'

Andrew nodded. 'Yes — and we discussed his interest in medical research. It's my belief that Simon's very gifted, Mrs Dean. I think you and your husband should think very seriously about moving him from the school he's at and sending him to one better equipped to deal with his needs.'

She gave a short laugh. 'You make it sound like a handicap.'

'It is. It's every bit as much of a handicap being too clever as not being clever enough. Our aim should be to help all children reach their potential. Slow children or those with a mental impairment get educational provision as a matter of right. Unfortunately the more able children get told to be good and are expected to behave even when, like Simon, they're bored rigid.

'Now, I think I should refer you to the educational psychologist for tests, and after that I think you may have some tough decisions to make.'

'Such as?'

Andrew shrugged. 'I don't know your personal circumstances, but I would hazard a guess that the only sort of school you'll find for him will be an independent prep school specifically geared to high achievers. It may even mean boarding, but that might be preferable to him going totally off the rails. I suspect, though, that he'd easily get a scholarship.'

'Good grief,' Mrs Dean said slowly. 'I thought he had a food allergy or a brain tumour or something.'

Andrew smiled his reassurance. 'Nothing like that. He's just bored out of his skull. Ask the receptionist to make you an appointment with the educational psychologist for as soon as possible, and in the meantime take him down to the library and indulge his interests.'

Aftr he had showed the astonished Mrs Dean out, he called Jennifer over to him and shut the door behind her. She was defensive and wouldn't look at him, and he wanted to pull her into her arms and hug her, but of course he couldn't. He stuffed his hands in his pockets to keep them away from her.

'I'm sorry,' he apologised gruffly. 'It's been one of those days. I had no right to take it out on you.'

She looked at him, and the hurt showed clearly in her eyes. 'It doesn't matter,' she said quietly, but he knew it did. It was no use explaining that it was meeting Nick that had thrown him. It would look like a bid for sympathy, and she had enough troubles without him laying a guilt trip on her on his behalf.

Instead he told her about Simon Dean, and by the time she showed in the next patient their relationship was almost back to normal.

And if they were a little distant with each other, then that was probably no bad thing. It would make it easier for them both when she went back to Nick.

He realised with a heavy heart that he had already virtually conceded defeat.

In contrast to Andrew's sober withdrawal, Nick was bouncy and cheerful that evening.

'I take it it's going well,' she said drily, and he chuckled.

'Am I so transparent? They've got a great team there. I think I'll learn a lot.'

She shot him a teasing glance. 'In a provincial hospital? Surely not!'

His mouth tilted in a wry grin. 'Amazing, isn't it? However, I didn't come here to talk about work. How's my favourite lady?'

His favourite lady was depressed, but she wasn't about to tell him that. 'OK. Tim's cold is getting better, thank goodness.'

'Is he asleep?'

'I think so — why?'

His eyes smouldered slightly. 'Because it means I've got you to myself.'

They were standing in the kitchen, just inches apart, and before she could protest he had closed the gap and lowered his mouth to hers.

Even after so long, the contact was comfortingly familiar, and for a few stunned seconds she swayed against him. It would be so easy just to let go. . .

His arms tightened around her, pressing her closer to him, and with a shock she felt his reaction to their embrace and twisted away. Taking a few shaken steps back, she touched her hand to her mouth, watching him warily.

'No?' he asked, softly.

She dragged in a ragged breath, shocked at how easy it would have been to surrender to the familiar pattern. She shook her head, partly in denial, partly to clear it for rational thought. 'Nick, I thought I told you — '

'You told me you wouldn't go to bed with me yet. I never said I wouldn't try and change your mind.'

But he took her rejection good-naturedly, helping her with the coffee and then carrying the tray through to the sitting-room.

'I annoyed you this afternoon, didn't I?' he said unexpectedly a few minutes later.

'You guessed?' she said wryly.

He laughed softly. 'I'm sorry. I didn't mean to be rude, but he is a little anal-retentive, isn't he?'

'You're disgusting,' she scolded, but he was grinning cheekily and she relented.

'It's very difficult for him.'

'How's he taking it?'

She didn't know how to answer. In truth, she didn't know how he was taking it. Apart from his uncharacteristic temper this afternoon, he had been enormously reasonable, offering her a shoulder to cry on and a willing ear whenever she needed it — not that she intended to take him up on it, it didn't seem fair, but he didn't seem to be making any attempt to compete with Nick. Perhaps he was simply relieved to be given a get-out from a proposal he had made in haste.

But there had been that kiss, the night she had told him Nick was coming back — brief, to be sure, and lacking the blatant sexuality of Nick's embrace, but packed with emotion. She had been shocked by the force of feeling she had felt bottled up inside him, even in the few short seconds it had lasted, but then he had gone, leaving her wondering if she had simply imagined it all.

Perhaps she had.

'I don't know how he's taking it,' she told Nick now.

'Lying down, I should say. He's hardly rising to the challenge,' Nick said drily, and made himself comfortable, one leg thrown with lazy casualness over the arm of the chair.

It was a consciously sexy pose, and she looked away, refusing to allow herself to be affected by it and by the charismatic smile on his handsome face.

'Because he didn't stoop to trading insults with you this afternoon?'

Nick laughed. 'Is that what I was doing? Trading insults?'

She looked at him then, the cocky grin, the twinkling eyes, and shook her head despairingly. 'Weren't you?'

He chuckled. 'Perhaps just a tad.'

She grew serious. 'Please don't bait him deliberately, Nick. I have a great deal of respect for him both professionally and as a friend. However you feel, he's done nothing to deserve your derision.'

Nick straightened. 'How was calling him the competition derisory?'

'Your body language is very expressive, Nick. He'd have to be blind and retarded not to see the challenge.'

'He didn't respond.'

'Perhaps because he felt it was beneath him to scrap over me as if I were a bone.'

'Like I said, a stuffed shirt — sorry! Sorry, I was only joking!' He shifted and grinned again. 'What were you saying about my body language?'

'No — watch my lips — N-O.'

He laughed softly. 'Aw, shucks.'

'Go on, out. I have to take Tim shopping tomorrow. He's managed to get the knee out of his school trousers.'

'Well, hooray! Normal behaviour at last.'

She sat back with a sigh. 'Nick, if this is not going to be a totally pointless exercise, you are going to have to do something pretty damn drastic about your attitude. Tim doesn't need your juvenile sense of humour, nor do I, and Andrew certainly doesn't.'

His face sobered instantly. 'Jen, I'm sorry. I'm just edgy, I guess. There's so much at stake.'

'For all of us — remember that. We're all walking a knife-edge at the moment, Andrew included.'

'Is he going to be a constant factor in our conversation?' Nick asked harshly. 'You said you weren't that involved with him.'

She looked him dead in the eye. 'No, you said that, not me.'

Nick gave a derisory snort. 'You didn't correct me. If he'd meant that much to you, you would have told me to get stuffed. And what about him? He doesn't seem in a hurry to challenge my presence here with you. Are you sure about his motives? Does he love you?'

'Well, I. . .'

'Has he said so?'

Jennifer hesitated, unable to lie. 'No. No, he hasn't.'

'Perhaps he just sees his life oozing away from him, and you and Tim represent an instant family. After all, he's hardly one of the world's Lotharios. Let's face it, anyone of that age who isn't married already is either gay or seriously flawed. Perhaps no one else will have him.'

She felt her temper rising again, but so did Nick.

He flung up his hands in self-defence. 'I'm sorry, I didn't mean to criticise. It was just an observation. Forget it.'

But she couldn't. Nick left, with a brief brush of his lips over her cheek, and she cleared away the coffee things and stood in the kitchen, looking out over the lights of the town and pondering on Nick's words.

Was that why Andrew had proposed, because his life was oozing away, as Nick put it? Even she had admitted that it was hardly going to be a marriage founded on passion — unlike the early days of her marriage to Nick.

But they had been head over heels in love. Had been. And if love was what was missing from her relationship with Andrew, it was also missing from her relationship with Nick now, because, despite the familiarity, his kiss earlier on had left her cold. But then, the passion had died in their marriage quite early on, as soon as Tim was on the way. At first she had thought it was because he was tired, then because he didn't find her swollen body attractive. Finally she was forced to admit that whatever the reason she was actually relieved.

Perhaps she just wasn't a very passionate person any more—but then, that weekend she had stayed with Andrew. . .

Hormones. Just because she was currently celibate didn't mean her body had shut down. It was natural, but meaningless.

So why didn't her body react like that to Nick's? Habit? Familiarity?

Contempt? a little voice whispered.

With a heavy sigh, she flicked off the kitchen light and made her way to bed, none the wiser.

CHAPTER SIX

NICK spent most of the weekend at the hospital, ostensibly to read up on the patients' notes, but mainly to keep himself out of Jen's way.

He'd pushed her too hard last night, from grabbing her in the kitchen to sowing the seeds of doubt about Andrew's feelings for her.

It was a little underhanded, because three seconds in the man's company had given him enough information to know that he thought the world of Jen.

He also realised that Andrew had no intention of standing between him and Jen. The man's integrity should have made Nick feel better. Instead, it made him feel worse, because it wasn't a fair fight.

Hell. That wasn't what it was about, and anyway, Tim was the real issue here—his elusive son, whose personality was totally alien to Nick. He wondered if their relationship would have been any better if he'd stuck it out, but the rows with Jen had become intolerable and he'd been too immature to stay and sort out their problems.

Two years of bed-hopping later, boredom and the AIDS scare had brought him to his senses—that and his thirtieth birthday looming on the horizon. All his friends were marrying and settling down, going for the very things he'd thrown away.

He'd spent two more years devoting himself to medicine and trying to sort out his feelings, and had finally come to the conclusion that he'd been a bloody fool.

Jen was beautiful, their son was an enigma to him, and both were out of reach.

And now he'd left it too late. She was clearly much more involved with this guy than he'd imagined, and, just to rub salt in the wound, Tim evidently thought the sun shone out of Andrew's left ear.

It was going to be a long and uphill struggle to woo them both, but woo them he would, if it took all his skill and ingenuity, because he had suddenly come to his senses and realised what he'd thrown away.

And if Andrew was going to be a magnanimous fool and hand them to him on a plate, then he'd be a worse fool not to grab the chance with both hands.

He'd just have to grow used to the prick of his conscience. After all, it was hardly his fault that Andrew had fallen for Jen.

But he would have to stop running the guy down for no good reason and trying to convince her that he was some kind of manufacturer's seconds. After all, there could be umpteen reasons why he hadn't married. He wondered idly why Andrew hadn't told Jen that he loved her. Strange, that, and yet another reason to be grateful to his adversary.

Poor bloody fool.

It seemed to Jennifer that the following days and weeks were composed of tiptoeing on eggshells. Tim discovered that his father would do almost anything that he asked, and practised his budding skills as a manipulator almost as a daily entertainment.

Nick was kept busy by a department that ran flat-out

to diminish its waiting-lists and treat particularly the elderly and children as soon as possible. He was tired, often unreasonable, and always at the flat.

By the middle of his first week Jennifer decided she was going to have to charge him housekeeping. She decided instead, at the last minute, to tell him not to darken their door unless he was fed, except by invitation.

'But I want to see Tim,' he said reasonably, 'and if I eat here, I can kill two birds with one stone and save time.'

'Fine,' Jennifer told him, 'you come for supper, you cook it — but not steak and chips!'

He grinned ruefully and agreed a compromise. He would eat with them every other night, providing the meal.

'Except Saturday. You'll need a babysitter; I'm taking you out.'

Saturday was the night of Michael and Clare Barrington's send-off before they flew to America, ready to sail *Henrietta* back to England. Jennifer had already promised the evening to Andrew, and although Nick was now back on the scene she had told Andrew she would still like to go with him, if that was what he wanted. A little reluctantly, he had agreed, so she wasn't about to pull out now. Nick would have to take her out another night.

'I'm sorry,' she told him now, 'I'm already going out.'

Nick stiffened. 'Who with?'

'Andrew.'

He positively bristled. 'Jen, I thought we were having another go at our relationship?'

'We are, but this was arranged ages ago, and I can't let him down. Don't worry, I'll be good.'

He muttered something suggestive under his breath, and she glared at him.

'You can trust me, you know.'

'Sorry, I know I can. And I can certainly trust him — he's too much of a gentleman to take advantage of you.'

He managed to make it sound like an insult. Jennifer opened her mouth to remonstrate with him, and he held up his hand and shook his head. 'I'm sorry. Forget it. You go out with the boyfriend, and I'll try and behave.'

'You do that,' she advised crisply. 'The practice will be good for you.'

In fact, he had a chance to practise his behaviour before the weekend.

It was the following day at the CF clinic, and Jackie Long, the girl with the pseudomonas infection who had missed her appointment a fortnight before, had come in — courtesy of the Hospital Car Service. Apparently the farm was isolated, they had no transport and Jackie's knee had been playing up so she had been unable to walk the mile to the bus stop.

Her chest was clear this time, since the GP had given her the antibiotics Andrew had prescribed over the phone to him, and he was more concerned about her knee.

It was swollen just below the patella, on the front of the tibial tuberosity, and was clearly inflamed and very painful to touch.

'Looks sore. Have you been doing a lot of exercise?'

Andrew asked her, running his hands gently over the leg.

She nodded. 'Mum and I have been doing this Step Reebok thing at home to a tape — well, we can't get to the village for the classes, but a friend taught us what to do and we were doing it every day — I thought it would be good for my lungs, but then my knee got sore and I had to give up.'

Andrew cocked his head on one side. In the distance, Jennifer heard Nick's familiar laugh.

'I think we could do with an orthopaedic opinion — would you mind, Sister?'

She returned his smile. 'Back in a mo.'

Nick was behind the reception desk, telling an outrageously funny story to the secretary and clinic receptionist. Janet was clutching her sides, Beattie, the domestic assitant, had tears running down her face, and he clearly had the attention of at least half the parents.

She let him finish, waited for the laughter to fade and then smiled icily.

'If you've finished strutting your stuff, Mr Davidson, Dr Barrett would like an orthopaedic opinion.'

The laughter dying from his eyes, he shrugged away from the filing cabinet and walked towards her, one brow elegantly raised.

'Is that a fact, Sister Davidson? And what, pray, am I supposed to be looking at?'

'I could dump you in it, but I believe I'll be kind this once,' she told him. 'I suspect it's Osgood-Schlatter Disease.'

'A knee.'

'No, a hip.'

He shot her a dry look. 'Give me a break, Jen, I'm not that inept!'

She laughed softly. 'Just checking. Patient's called Jackie Long.'

'Right.'

He opened the door, greeted Andrew and Mrs Long, and then turned to Jackie.

'Hello, young lady. I believe you've got a sore knee — is that right?'

Jackie, small for her age as CF sufferers often were but nonetheless afflicted with hormones, blushed and batted her eyelashes. 'Yes — it's this one,' she told him in what was almost a simper, and hitched her skirt unnecessarily high.

He didn't turn a hair, but giving his whole attention to her knee, he looked first, then touched, then asked her to hop on to the examination couch and lie on her back with her knees bent up.

Then, putting one hand under her thigh and the other over her shin, he asked her to try to straighten her leg.

She did so, and winced as the patellar tendon took the strain.

'Ow.'

'Sore?'

She nodded.

'What about the other one?'

He repeated the procedure, but found nothing wrong.

While he straightened her legs and rocked the knee joints in turn, he asked about her exercise pattern, nodded when she told him about the Step Reebok workouts and then told her to get down.

'Looks like a classic Osgood-Schlatter,' he said to Andrew. 'We can verify it with X-ray, and then treat accordingly. Would you like to explain, or shall I?'

Andrew waved a hand. 'Be my guest.'

Nick's smile was wry. 'Thank you. Technically, it's a traction injury of the patellar tendon, caused typically by over-use. In other words, you've done too much too hard, and the place on your shin where your thigh muscle connects via your knee-cap is inflamed and sore and needs rest. Sometimes it clears up quickly, sometimes it takes longer, but it's very common in girls and boys of your age, and may well happen in time to the other knee too. The best thing about it is that it's a self-limiting condition — you'll grow out of it at fourteen or so, when your bones stop growing, so it won't go on for ever or do you any permanent harm.

'Now, this looks pretty sore, so I suspect it will take quite a bit of rest to get it back to normal, but the first thing to do is get a photo of the inside just so we're absolutely sure. Once we know, then the physiotherapist here can advise you on other forms of exercise which will keep your lungs moving without affecting your knees, just until the condition settles. OK?'

Jackie nodded, and Nick turned to Andrew. 'Can you give her a topical NSAID like Traxam gel, for instance, unless it's contraindicated by other drugs? Four times a day, just until it settles, and repeat in short courses as necessary — paracetamol if she needs it, and icepacking for a few minutes several times a day if it feels hot — feel it with the back of your fingers, they're more sensitive than the front. And you might find wearing shoes with squishy soles helps — trainers or running shoes are ideal OK?'

He smiled at Jackie, winked at Jennifer and left, promising to check the X-ray and phone through the result.

After the Longs had left clutching their X-ray request, Andrew leant back in his chair and eyed Jennifer thoughtfully. 'Did you tell him?'

She smiled. 'I think he might have guessed anyway, but yes, I did.'

Andrew grinned. 'I should hope he would; it was a classic. He was good with her, though, the little flirt. Did you see the way she batted those baby blues at him?'

'He seems to have that effect on women,' Jennifer said drily, turning away to straighten the blanket on the couch so that she didn't see Andrew's jaw tighten. All except me, she could have added, and, if she had, she might have eased the dart of pain that stabbed through him.

Saturday night loomed large and menacing on the horizon. She knew it was going to be a very fancy affair, and had nothing to wear that was suitable. By Saturday, she admitted she would have to go shopping for something new. Nick and Tim were out for the morning, and so she abandoned the housework to its own devices and combed the town for that certain something.

She found it — at over three hundred pounds, and dismissed it instantly.

Scaling down, she went to a shop that specialised in Indian silks and found a long swirly skirt in deep royal blue that skimmed her ankles, and teamed it with a tiny camisole with spaghetti straps in the same wonderfully soft washed silk fabric. A broad gold leather belt finished it off, and she resigned herself to the same old strappy black evening sandals she had had for years. She had already spent far more than enough. Still, the overall effect was very feminine. She just hoped it wouldn't be cold, because it would look wonderful with her duffle coat over the top!

She bathed and washed her hair, and then while Tim was eating his supper she finger-dried her hair hanging over the edge of the bed to give it body. It was still the same old reddish brown, but with a little more eye make-up than usual, a soft coral lipstick and a touch of blusher, she thought she would pass muster. She slipped into the dress and top, realising with horror that there was no way she could wear an ordinary bra and she didn't have a strapless one. Still, there were tucks across the top edge of the blouse that almost covered her breasts, and provided she didn't jiggle about too much it would hopefully be OK. They were a little too full, and normally she wouldn't have considered going without a bra, especially not since Tim, but she had no choice. With the addition of a soft printed wool shawl her sister had sent her for Christmas last year draped artfully round her shoulders, she felt a little more secure. That decided, she stood back for one last critical look in the mirror.

The belt certainly emphasised her tiny waist, and the sparkle of the glitter tights below the hem of the skirt seemed to find an echo in her eyes. She realised with surprise that she was looking forward to the evening, even though it was only Andrew who was taking her out. Still, it was a long time since she had been out to a function like this, and why shouldn't she enjoy herself?

At seven-thirty on the dot her babysitter arrived, followed shortly by Andrew looking very impressive in a dinner suit and bow tie. She had a sudden moment of panic that she might be underdressed for the occasion.

'Will I do?' she asked lightly, giving him a little twirl that disguised her last-minute nerves.

If she was worred about his reaction to her appearance, she need not have bothered. He ran his eye over her and frowned at the printed wool shawl flung around her shoulders. 'You look fine. Will you be warm enough?' he asked gruffly. 'It's a fairly mild night, but I'd hate you to get cold.'

She ignored a little twinge of disappointment. Had she expected Andrew to go into raptures over her outfit? Of course not! 'I'll be all right,' she dismissed with a little smile. 'If I get cold I can always borrow your jacket.'

'I think you might get lost inside it,' he said wryly, and, handing over her bag, he held the door for her and escorted her down to the car.

'I'm sorry—a diesel four-wheel-drive is hardly appropriate for Cinderella, but I have washed it,' he apologised ruefully as he helped her in.

She threw him a warm smile. 'I'll forgive you—you'd look ridiculous behind the wheel of a Porsche.'

He laughed. 'I don't think I'd *get* behind the wheel of a Porsche—there's too much of me. All set?'

She nodded, and he shut the door and went round, swinging himself easily up behind the wheel. 'Right, let's go and party.'

He sounded so dismal that Jennifer laughed.

He shot her something halfway between a grin and a grimace. 'I hate functions.'

'So why are you going?'

He shrugged. 'Because I admire Michael very much. Because it's a good cause and we all know I'm a pushover, and because it's a chance to have you to myself.' His grin took any suggestiveness out of his remark, and she smiled back. Whatever the reason, it was good to see him again outside work, to have a chance to forget her problems and dance the night away without Nick watching over her.

She was mistaken. Almost the first person she saw as they arrived at the prestigious country club was Nick.

'What's he doing here?' she murmured aloud.

Andrew glanced over to where Nick was slouched elegantly against the bar, chatting up a pretty girl.

'He's covering for Michael. I suppose it's only to be expected.'

'Of course — how silly of me.'

Andrew eyed her closely. 'Does it matter? We could leave, if you like,' he said, ever thoughtful, and she shook her head.

'No — no, of course not. Anyway, you can't get out of it that easily.'

He chuckled. 'Am I so transparent?'

A circulating waiter paused beside them with a tray full of glasses, and Andrew took two and handed her one.

'What is it?' she asked.

He sniffed. 'Something fizzy — champenoise!'

The bubbles tickled her nose, and she resolved to forget about Nick lurking in the background and enjoy herself. Tucking her hand into the crook of Andrew's solid and reassuring arm, she sipped her wine and looked up at his solemn face.

'Let's go and find Michael and Clare and wish them well — and try and enjoy it!'

His smile was wry. 'I'll do my best,' he murmured.

They threaded their way through the crowd, and after a while they saw Michael's blond head thrown back in laughter.

'He's always so cheerful,' she said wonderingly. 'You'd think, losing his leg like that and then Clare having that ectopic pregnancy, he'd be morose and unhappy, but he never is.'

'I didn't know about Clare. How sad.'

'I hope they aren't superstitious. I'd be worried about the third thing.'

'Mmm. Makes you wonder about this trip.'

She laughed. 'I think this trip is madness anyway, but who's going to listen to me? They both seem keen enough, and he's a very good sailor. They're hoping to raise thousands for PHAB and RADAR.'

Andrew nodded. 'They'll do it, too, I have no doubt. He's done a tremendous amount already for disabled children. He's a fantastic example to them, as well — I don't think there's anything he won't tackle.'

'Except the ironing — Clare says he'll do anything to get out of it.'

Andrew grinned. 'We have that in common, then.'

Jennifer laughed. 'She says that's the only reason he wanted to marry her, so she would do the ironing. . .'

Her smile faltered, and her eyes meshed with Andrew's. The doubts Nick had sown in her mind came back to haunt her, and she knew they must show in her eyes. Was that why Andrew had wanted her? Not for the ironing, particularly, but just to carry the household chores?

And why had she agreed to marry him? For security, for peace of mind, for companionship?

She looked away, disgusted with herself. Who was she to judge anyone for their motives? Everyone used everyone else. Nobody was any different.

She felt suddenly jaded and very, very tired.

'Do you really want to speak to them, or shall we go and find a quiet corner and sit down?' His voice was soft in her ear, and she felt the warm brush of his breath tease the strands of hair against her cheek.

'Sit down,' she replied, suddenly breathless. Already the room felt airless and hot, and she had an overwhelming need to take off her wrap. But there was the problem of the camisole top.

She glanced around. There were women in far less — low cut bodices, thigh-high splits — and anyway, it was only Andrew, and he'd seen it all before.

His hand on the hollow of her spine added to the warmth, and when he settled her in a chair near the edge of the dance-floor, she was relieved to take the wrap off and drape it over the back of the chair.

As she turned back her eyes meshed with Andrew's for an endless moment, and then he looked away.

'Colourful crowd.'

She swallowed. 'Yes, they are.'

Now what?

'How are the cats?'

He eased back in the chair with a little sigh. 'Fine. The kittens are four weeks old tomorrow.'

'Is that all?'

Four weeks since she had stayed with him, since she had lain in his arms and begged him to make love to her — and what a disastrous mistake that would have been!

She took a gulp of her drink and set it down again slightly unsteadily.

'Tim would love to see them again.'

'You must bring him over.'

'Yes.'

His eyes tracked rapidly over her, and he looked away again. 'We could dance.'

'Do you want to?'

He gave a short laugh. 'It's not really my thing.'

'Nor mine. Nick loves to dance — he makes John Travolta look arthritic.'

Andrew chuckled. 'This I have to see.'

'Oh, you will. Any opportunity to make an exhibition of himself,' she replied, and was shocked at the bitterness in her voice. What was the matter with her? Surely the least she could be was loyal?

'Penny for them.'

She shook her head. 'I was just. . .'

'Feeling guilty?'

She met his eyes, startled. 'Am I so obvious?'

His mouth lifted in a gentle smile. 'No — I just know how your mind works.'

Just then the MC interrupted the music to welcome everyone, and handed the microphone over to Michael Barrington.

He thanked everyone for their generous support, told them what had been raised and how much more was in the pipeline, and then when he could finally get a word in edgeways over the thunderous applause and cheers he instructed them to have a good time.

There was a buffet supper laid out in the dining-room, after which the dancing began to warm up.

Jennifer and Andrew sat back, relieved of the burden of conversation by the loudness of the music, and watched the gyrations of the couples on the floor.

Nick, in fine form, exhausted his partner and found another, then another, then the first again.

'Lord, he's fit,' Andrew commented after almost an hour.

'Constitution of an ox,' she replied, and took another swig of her drink. Of course, if they were married he would expect her to be there with him, leaping and thrashing about among the music like a mad thing.

The music changed, slowing to a more gentle rhythm, and Nick appeared at her side, bowing slightly to Andrew and smiling a lop-sided smile as he bore her away.

His arms closed round her, easing her against his body, and she felt the firm pressure of his hand against her spine, kneading gently.

'You look beautiful—sexy and mysterious.'

She flushed, and then remembered that this was Nick, who threw away compliments like confetti. 'What do you want?' she asked candidly, and he laughed huskily in her ear.

'A wild night of passion—what else?'

'Fool.'

He sighed, and his hand slid down over her bottom and back to her waist. 'Extraordinary, isn't it, the way we get in such a lather over a couple of yards of worm-spit?'

'Pardon?' She stopped in her tracks, and his arms and soft laugh urged her on.

'Silk. Absurd that it should be so erotic.'

His hand slid lower and smoothed round her hip and back, coming to rest just below her waist.

'God, you're lovely, Jen. I mean it. Come back with me tonight. Let me make love to you till the dawn touches the sky and our bodies plead for mercy.'

She laughed, and a rueful smile touched his lips.

'No?'

'Go to hell, darling,' she said softly.

'You're cruel to me.'

'Rubbish. You're drunk.'

'Only very slightly. Not too drunk to do you justice. God, you're sexy tonight. That top is something else.'

She flushed again, and eased away, embarrassed now.

'I think I'd like to sit down.'

'Finish the dance.'

'Only if you're good.'

'I'll be fantastic——'

'Nick. . .'

'Sorry.' He eased her closer again, but other than that managed to behave himself for the duration of the dance.

Andrew watched, his temper foul, as Nick ran his hands possessively over Jennifer's body. Damn the man, how dared he behave like that in public?

Trapped by the side of the dance-floor, condemned by his conscience to mineral water so he couldn't even seek the oblivion of drink, he was forced to watch.

She laughed at one point, and he felt jealousy like a

knife twist in his gut. Then she said something to Nick, and his hands settled down and he seemed to behave.

At the end he returned her to Andrew with a mocking smile and left, immediately swept into another dance by a blonde with legs up to her armpits, who sidled against him in a blatantly sexual fashion.

He was clearly not a bit fazed by the woman's behaviour, but slid his hands over her bottom and pulled her harder against him as they moved round the floor.

Andrew's mouth tightened, and Jennifer covered his hand and shook her head.

'He's only trying to make me jealous because I refused to sleep with him tonight.'

The knife turned again. Tonight — as distinct from any other night, or was tonight to be the first time? Hardly. Nick wouldn't let the grass grow under his feet. Nausea clawed at his gut, and he watched as Nick slid one thigh between the woman's and rocked against her.

Bastard. His behaviour now made Andrew's fists itch in a totally uncharacteristic urge to hit him. So he was trying to make her jealous?

'Two can play at that game,' he muttered under his breath, and stood up. 'Let's dance.'

Jennifer looked up at Andrew, puzzled. He seemed quite calm, and yet she knew he was angry. His grip on her arm was gentle but about as yielding as granite, and he urged her firmly to her feet and into his arms.

There was none of Nick's insidious hand-sliding over her bottom, just a warm, firm hand in the small of her back and his other hand cradling hers against the solid wall of his chest as they moved slowly amongst the other dancers.

The floor was more crowded now, and he eased her closer and tucked her head under his chin, so that the steady beat of his heart was under her ear and his warm, subtly masculine fragrance curled round her, invading all her senses. The back of his hand grazed the swell of her breast, and she was suddenly, vividly aware of his body, the breadth of his shoulders, the depth of his chest, the light brush of his hard thighs against hers as they moved in time to the music. She was aware of his strength, his muscles like seasoned oak, rippling as he swayed, and of his gentleness, the light touch of his hand against her spine, the protective way he cradled the other against his chest. He had the power to snap her in two if he chose to, and yet he held her as if she was the most precious thing he had ever touched.

Suddenly, unexpectedly, she wanted to cry.

Nick's tap on her shoulder was unwelcome and intrusive, but Andrew released her and she was swept away in Nick's arms.

As he turned, she glimpsed Andrew standing stock still in the middle of the crowd, looking after them, and his eyes were empty.

'You're behaving abominably,' she told Nick angrily. 'You're making a total exhibition of yourself, and I refuse to be dragged into your silly games. If you really mean what you said about having another chance, you're going to have to do a damn sight better than this!'

And with that she spun out of his arms and searched for Andrew in the crowd.

She spotted him just as he reached their table, and squeezed her way between the couples until she reached him.

'Andrew, would you mind very much taking me home?' she asked unsteadily.

'Of course not.' He was on his feet instantly, handing her her wrap and bag, and with one arm curled protectively round her shoulders and a look of thunder in his eyes, he led her to the door.

At her flat, she asked him in for coffee but he declined.

'Please,' she pressed. 'I really don't want to be alone. It isn't late—I won't keep you long.'

He studied her for a long moment, then nodded. 'OK—just a quick one, though. I want to pop into the hospital on my way home.'

Her babysitter was surprised to see her back so early. She paid her until one, although it was only half-past eleven, and then after showing her out she closed the door and sighed.

'Don't let him hurt you,' Andrew said gently. 'He just needs to grow up a bit.'

'He's always needed to do that,' she said bitterly. 'Why did I think he'd actually managed it this time?'

'Come here.'

Andrew's voice was soft and husky, and his arms looked endlessly inviting. She walked into them and laid her head against his chest.

'I'm sorry I spoilt your evening,' she mumbled into his immaculate white shirtfront.

'You didn't,' he murmured quietly. 'Have I told you how lovely you look tonight?'

She shook her head. 'Nick said it was amazing that

we all got so worked up over a few yards of worm spit.'

'Worm spit?'

'He was talking about my outfit.'

His arms tightened fractionally and she felt the warm spread of his fingers against her spine, caressing the silk. 'Philistine,' he murmured. 'You look beautiful.'

Her heart glowed at the praise. Funny how different it made her feel when it was sincere. 'Thank you.'

'You're welcome.'

His breath fanned warmly over her cheek, and she felt the soft graze of his chin against her forehead.

'I must go.'

'But you haven't had a drink!'

She leant back in his arms and looked up at him, surprising a look of longing in his eyes.

'Andrew?' she whispered, and then his lips brushed hers and he released her.

'Goodnight, my love,' he said gently but firmly, and he let himself out, closing the door quietly behind him.

She listened to the sound of his receding footsteps, and then went to the window, watching as he crossed the car park and swung himself behind the wheel of his car. As the lights came on and he drove away, she stared after him, her face grave.

He was nothing more to her than a friend, surely? A very dear friend, it was true, but still no more than that.

So why, then, as she watched his tail-lights fade into the night, did she feel this strange and disquieting sense of loss?

CHAPTER SEVEN

ANDREW trudged wearily through the hospital, his thoughts still on the child in ITU. He would find the houseman on duty and fill him in on the current state of play, and then go home for what was left of the night.

Not that he expected to sleep. Images of Jennifer would prevent that, and not for the first time. Ever since the dance he had had trouble sleeping, and when he did still she came to haunt him, with her clear grey eyes like a rainwashed sky and her soft, supple body that called to his in the long, lonely hours of the night.

He had tried to distance himself from her in the week that had passed, but, although outwardly he might have appeared indifferent, inwardly he ached every time he heard her voice.

Davidson, of course, was always on the scene, endlessly cheerful, and she always seemed to brighten up when he came within range — although, come to think about it, he had wondered on occasions if it was a forced cheer. He'd dismissed the thought as clutching at straws, but he didn't like to ask. She could always come to him if she wanted to talk about it. He'd made that abundantly clear — and regretted it ever since.

He hoped the blasted man was making her happy, because as sure as eggs he was playing havoc with Andrew's own life.

With a weary sigh, he turned into the corridor of the

residence and made his way towards his houseman's room. He'd been around half an hour ago. With any luck he would still be awake.

His hand was raised to tap on the door when he saw Nick emerging from a room a few doors down, followed by a blonde — the same blonde, if he was not mistaken, who had smeared herself all over him like treacle at the dance.

She wound her arms round his neck and kissed him hungrily, then reluctantly released him.

'Bye for now,' she purred softly, then turned back to the room and closed the door as Nick walked away.

Andrew's hand fell to his side and he moved swiftly down the corridor, rage boiling inside him.

'Davidson?'

Nick's head came up. 'Hi. Were you looking for me?'

'We need to talk,' he said tersely.

Nick shrugged. 'My room?'

'I would prefer it to the corridor, and in view of what I have to say I think you probably would, too.'

Nick's brows quirked, but he turned without a word and led the way to another part of the residence, opening his door and showing Andrew in with exaggerated courtesy. He closed the door behind them and turned to Andrew with a wary smile.

'What can I do for you?'

'You can stop messing Jennifer around.'

'What?'

'Don't play games with me,' Andrew growled.

Nick returned his level stare for a moment, then looked away. 'You saw,' he said flatly.

'I saw.'

'Oh. Drink?'

Andrew glared at him. 'No. What the hell do you think you're playing at?'

Nick laughed uncomfortably. 'Look, it was nothing — just meaningless recreation. It won't lead anywhere —— '

'Too damn right. Hospitals are small communities. Word — especially scurrilous, muck-laden word — travels like lightning. What do you think it'll do to Jennifer to hear you've been playing around with that unscrupulous tart?'

'Oh, come on, we only had a drink in the residence bar — anybody would think I'd slept with her.'

'Haven't you?'

Nick returned his level stare coldly. 'As a matter of fact, I haven't — but even if I had, I can't see what the hell it is to you.'

Andrew took a step closer, and hunched over Nick, his control frayed to breaking point. 'Oh, can't you?' he said, his voice dangerously quiet. 'Well, let me explain. When Jennifer told me you were coming back and wanted another shot at your marriage, I was prepared to stand back and give you both a chance, because I believe very strongly in the sanctity of marriage. I also believe that your son needs a father, and that your wife needs a partner, someone to lean on, someone to share life's joys and sorrows. For their sakes I was prepared to stand back and give you a chance, but get this —— ' he stabbed Nick menacingly with his forefinger ' — I owe you nothing. Do you read me? Nothing. You mess her about, and you'll have me to deal with. I won't have her hurt. Is that clear?'

'As crystal.' Nick's eyes blazed blue with cold rage.

'Now you get this. I don't need a keeper, Barrett. Mind your own damn business.'

'She is my business. And you'd better remember that.'

'What are you going to do?' Nick taunted. 'Break my legs?'

'I've heard worse ideas.'

Nick chuckled softly under his breath. 'You're unconvincing, Barrett. And Jennifer doesn't need a champion.'

Andrew met his eyes. 'No. What she needs is someone she can trust and respect, not an unfaithful bastard who doesn't take her love seriously.'

Nick opened his mouth, then shut it and turned away.

'Jen understands me.'

'Yes. She also hoped you would have changed with the years. For God's sake, grow up, Nick. She deserves better than that, and if you can't hack it, then butt out.'

'And leave her to you? No way.'

Andrew grabbed his shoulder and slammed him back against the wall, his control gone. 'This isn't a game, Davidson!' he growled. 'This is her life you're playing with? Damn it, man, don't you love her?'

Nick's eyes locked with Andrew's, and gradually the anger drained away, leaving hopelessness in its wake. He looked away.

'Yes, I love her,' he said quietly. 'I love her, but I can't seem to get through to her.'

'And you think playing around with that whore will help?'

'Pam's not a whore ——'

Andrew snorted. 'She has a reputation a mile wide — ask any of the surgical staff. She gets through men faster than the black plague.'

Nick's mouth lifted in a reluctant smile. 'I can believe it,' he said wryly, and then he sobered. 'Look, I only went out for a drink with her and that's as far as it's ever gone. That kiss was. . .nothing. I promise you it won't happen again.' He sighed and sat down heavily on the edge of the bed. 'I just felt like a little light-hearted fun. I don't want to hurt Jen, but sometimes she and Tim just seem like an alien species — do you know what I mean?'

Andrew looked at Nick, and knew exactly what he was saying. The man's mind was a total mystery to him. 'Yes, I know what you mean, but tangling with the likes of that scrub nurse is not the best way to understand them.'

'So what do you suggest?'

Andrew gave a snort of disbelieving laughter. 'Are you serious? You want me to tell you how to get through to her? Damn it, man, she was your wife!'

Nick rubbed his hand absently over his thigh. 'Yeah. It was a long time ago. She's changed.'

'Maybe she's grown up. Perhaps you should try it.'

In the thoughtful silence that followed, he let himself out and made his way to the exit. He was halfway home before he realised he still hadn't seen his houseman.

Nick was different. It was difficult to put her finger on why, but for the past few days he had seemed — more earnest, perhaps? As if he had suddenly pulled himself together and was making the first real attempt at a reconciliation.

Gone were the sexist remarks and the roaming hands, the throwaway comments and the cavalier attitude. In their place was a genuine attempt to talk to her, to find out what she wanted to do, what her interests were, how she felt about things.

For the first time, it seemed he was really making the effort to get to know her again.

Even Tim noticed it.

'Dad's changed,' he said one evening. 'He asked me what I wanted to eat tomorrow, and he didn't even pull a face.'

'What did you say?' she asked curiously, knowing how Tim had taken to winding Nick up.

'Squid.'

She couldn't keep her face straight. 'Tim, you are awful. It'll serve you right if he brings it.'

Tim grinned engagingly, looking suddenly and rarely like his father. 'I'll just have to pretend I feel sick.'

Jennifer laughed and rumpled his hair. 'Darling, that's very naughty. He's trying to fit in with us, you shouldn't tease him.'

'Yeah.' He looked thoughtful. 'Can you tell him when you see him tomorrow that I've changed my mind?'

'To what—snails?'

'Oh, yuck, gross! How about chicken tikka?'

She grinned. 'Perhaps I ought to let him bring squid, just to teach you a lesson!'

'Oh, Mum, no!' he pleaded, but she sent him off to bed in suspense. In fact she didn't see Nick until nearly five on Thursday afternoon. It had been a busy day and he passed through on his way from the orthopaedic clinic.

'Bring chicken tikka but tell him it's squid,' she instructed, and Nick threw back his head and laughed.

'Think I'll bring squid just to teach the little rascal. I'll see you later.'

His eyes were full of warmth, and she couldn't help but respond.

The smile was still on her lips when she went back into Andrew's office.

He was staring crossly at the computer screen in the corner, and turned to frown at her when she went in.

'Something funny?' he growled.

She told him about Tim winding Nick up, and his face softened. 'Are they getting on better?'

'They do seem to be. Oh, lord, I hope it works. It's been a source of such worry to me over the years, but — do you know, he's been different since the weekend? More — human, somehow. I wonder what brought it on — not that I wish to look a gift horse in the mouth, but it's almost as if he's feeling guilty.'

Andrew shrugged non-commitally and turned back to the screen. 'Maybe. Perhaps he realised he wasn't trying hard enough.'

'Well, he's certainly trying now.' Jennifer sighed and leant against the desk. 'Are you ready to see Anthony Craven?'

'Mmm.' He turned back from the screen and glanced at her. 'Have the plates come down from X-ray?'

'Yes — his lungs are clear, apparently.'

'Good. Right, wheel him in. I'd like to get away fairly promptly because the kittens'll be ravenous, and I've got to come back in later.'

'They can't be on solids yet!'

'They are — they're nearly six weeks old.'

Jennifer looked down into his warm, gentle eyes, remembering the weekend they had been born and the love she and Andrew had so nearly shared. 'Is it really that long?' she whispered pensively.

Something, some not-quite-forgotten fire, blazed deep in his eyes, and he looked away. 'Sometimes I think it seems far, far longer,' he murmured, and his voice was tinged with sadness.

'Oh, Andrew, I'm so sorry. . .'

She reached out and touched his arm, and felt the muscles clench beneath her fingertips. His hand over hers was hard and warm and comforting.

'Don't be,' he advised gruffly. 'Life's too short for regrets.'

He turned away, and she dropped her hand and walked to the door.

'I'll get Anthony.'

Andrew didn't get away as early as he would have liked, because Anthony Craven's parents, and especially his father, were concerned about their ability to cope with his physiotherapy and the constant juggling of the enzyme replacements he had to take in vast quantities with each meal.

He was also having difficulty at school with bullying because of all the pills he had to take during his meal at lunchtime, and because the mother worked until one she was unable to have him at home for lunch.

Andrew talked to them for ages, and they booked a session with the physiotherapist for more coaching on their percussive technique. Andrew also thought it might be a good idea, now Anthony was getting older, to try an expiration technique at lunchtime to save the school nurse having to do his physio, as that didn't seem to be too effective either.

Because he was late, Jennifer was late getting away too, and by the time she got to Tim her childminder was getting agitated.

She apologised and rushed them both back to the flat, quickly tidying up ready for Nick's arrival.

'Did you see him?' Tim asked worriedly, clearly panicking about the squid.

'We were busy all day,' she said evasively, and left him stewing. Do him good, she thought fondly, and Nick when he arrived continued the teasing right through to the moment when the food appeared on the table.

Tim's relief was comical, and in the shared laughter Jennifer saw at last the beginnings of a spirit of family unity which until then had been sadly lacking.

The evening was easier than in the past, and when Nick left after Tim was in bed asleep it was with a lingering kiss goodnight. How easy it would have been to let him stay, she thought as she closed the door behind him.

Not that his kiss had stirred any passion in her, but there was a tender warmth that with time and patience might have grown to become passion of a sort.

And anyway, passion was hardly the issue here, which was just as well because Nick had never been long on patience.

But for the first time she could see that a relationship with him might be possible.

It should have made her happy. Instead, the realisation that they were likely to get back together left her feeling strangely sad.

Andrew was away on Monday at a conference, and so she didn't see him until the Wednesday morning diabetic clinic.

Paul Downing was bubbling over with his visit to the zoo the weekend before.

'Where did you go?' Jennifer asked, expecting him to say one of the local zoos, but no, he had been to Whipsnade, and chattered throughout his consultation about each and every animal he had seen.

Andrew patiently listened, examined him, checked the height, weight and blood-sugar results in the notes and even managed to get in the odd question about his diet, quite without him being aware of it.

'Well, they seem to be coping better,' Andrew said after Jennifer showed the still-chattering child and his bemused mother out of the door.

'Nothing wrong with his enthusiasm, anyway,' she replied laughingly. 'What a chatterbox!'

'Maybe they'll settle down now and it'll all be all right. I take back everything I said about the spoilt little brat — he seems really to have enjoyed it.'

Their next patient, however, was definitely not enjoying life.

Suzanne Hooper, thinner still and hovering almost permanently on the brink of hypoglycaemia, was sullen, difficult to communicate with and clearly making no attempt to eat sufficient carbohydrate for her body's needs.

She told them she had cut down her insulin level so that she didn't have so many hypos, and when she told

Andrew the number of units she was having, he was appalled.

'Suzanne, that is clearly not enough to keep you alive,' he told her worriedly. 'Your last HbA result was far too low — you've been abusing yourself for much too long. You're going to suffer permanent damage if you don't co-operate.'

She rolled her eyes. 'Not you, too! I've got Mum and Dad on my case all day long, and that stupid pyschologist woman — none of you seem to be able to understand!'

'So talk to us. Explain,' he urged gently, but she went sullen and uncommunicative again and wouldn't talk.

He sent her out to the waiting-room and spoke at length to her worried mother, explaining that if Suzanne continued the way she was she was going to fade away before their eyes.

'If we can't halt this downward spiral soon, she'll have to come in and be put on a drip until we've got her stable again and back to her proper weight, but that isn't the real answer. I was hoping the clinical psychologist would be able to make some progress with her, but it doesn't seem to be working to date.'

'Oh, God, she's going to die, I know it,' Mrs Hooper said despairingly, and burst into tears.

Andrew laid a warm hand on her shoulder and let her cry for a moment, then gave her a handful of tissues.

'We'll give her another week. Let her see the psychologist next week as planned, and we'll review her progress. If there's no change, we'll admit her at the end of next week. I won't let her die, Mrs Hooper, not if I can avoid it. I'll move heaven and earth before I give up on her.'

'Thank you,' she murmured tearfully, and, mopping herself up, she gathered her things together and left.

'I hope you aren't making promises you can't keep,' Jennifer said quietly as the door closed.

Andrew met her eyes, his own serious. 'So do I,' he murmured, 'so do I.'

They were to find out only ten days later. . .

'Where's Lucy Banks?'

Andrew glanced up from the notes he was writing and set his pen down thoughtfully.

'In the ward. I admitted her last night with a deep-seated strep infection, and a query virus on top. She's in a hell of a mess.'

Jennifer perched on the edge of the desk, arms wrapped round the notes she was holding, and searched Andrew's worried face.

'Will she make it?'

He shrugged. 'Maybe this time. Not many more, that's for sure. She's had such a rotten summer, poor kid.'

'I thought we hadn't seen her very much down here,' Jennifer said slowly. 'It must be awful. Tim can be a little beast at times, but the thought of losing him. . .'

She broke off and shook her head.

'Suzanne Hooper's in, too. She had another hypo at school yesterday and came in so weak I've got her on a drip — against her better judgement, I might add.'

'I'll bet — has she pulled it out yet?'

He laughed. 'Only twice. Once she realised we could put it back in every time, and it hurt, she gave up.' He fiddled with his pen, giving it an inordinate amount of attention suddenly. 'How are you and Nick getting on?' he asked quietly.

'Oh, up and down. We had a bit of a row last night — rumour has it he's been seeing one of the theatre nurses——'

Andrew's pen sprayed ink all over the front of his white coat and across the notes. He swore uncharacteristically and grabbed a handful of tissues, blotting furiously at the notes. He seemed livid, his face tense and his movements jerky.

'What did he say?'

Jennifer eyed him curiously. 'He said it was nothing. Why? What have you heard?'

He continued blotting.

'Andrew?' she prodded.

'Not much,' he said tersely. 'I don't think there's anything in it. I know he's had a couple of drinks with one of the nurses, but——'

'Pam Slater?'

He sighed. 'Jennifer, it's nothing. It was weeks ago.'

She drew in a steadying breath. 'I knew he'd been up to something. You really would think after all he said I'd be able to trust him. . .'

Andrew lifted his head and searched her face with his gentle eyes. 'I think you can trust him,' he said quietly. 'I think it was harmless — done without thought, but blown up out of all proportion by the jungle drums. Ignore it.'

'I can't ignore it — Andrew, I've been there before.'

'Talk to him again,' he advised.

She sighed. 'I can't. He's taking Tim to his parents

for the weekend, and I won't see him except with Tim on Friday.'

Andrew eyed her thoughtfully. 'What are you doing over the weekend?'

She shrugged. 'Not a lot — why?'

'Just wondered — they're a little short-staffed on the ward over the weekend — at least for qualified staff. I thought maybe you might like the chance to do a bit of overtime — help pay for that computer you want to get Tim for Christmas.'

She looked doubtful for a moment. 'Do you think I could? It's ages since I did any ward work.'

He lifted a shoulder. 'Why not? Have a chat to Admin, ask — you can't lose anything.'

'Are you on call?'

He nodded. 'Mmm. It might help Suzanne Hooper if we were both around, too. Familiar faces and all that. Think about it.'

'I will — thanks.'

The idea grew on her over the afternoon, and in a sudden lull she rang the nursing officer and asked her if she would be able to put in any time.

'Wonderful!' she was told. 'We could really use you on a late on Saturday and early on Sunday — the other shifts aren't so bad, but on Saturday afternoon we've only got one staff nurse on, and she's not really senior enough to carry the ward in the evening. I know it's a rotten combination, but it would be such a help. We've got so many people off sick!'

So that was that. For the rest of the day she wondered what on earth she had done, but by the end of the following day she found she was really looking forward to her weekend on the wards.

And how much of that was due to Andrew being on call and how much to the opportunity for some real hands-on nursing again, she didn't care to analyse. Anyway, she didn't have much time to think, and the time she had was largely given to Nick. There was something she had to sort out before the weekend.

She had got all Tim's things ready the night before, so that when Nick arrived on Friday evening she had time to drag him into the kitchen for a quick word.

He looked puzzled. 'What is it?' he asked softly.

'Pam Slater,' she said briefly, and he closed his eyes and ran his hand over his face.

'Oh, darling——'

'Don't "darling" me! What happened? Exactly?'

'Exactly? I took her home after the dance and took her back to her room and left her there. A week later I ran into her in the bar and we had a drink together. I went back to her room, had a coffee, she tried to seduce me. I said no. I might as well not have done for all the bloody good it's done me. I kissed her goodnight and escaped.'

She eyed him thoughtfully. 'And that's all?'

'That's all. As God is my witness, I didn't sleep with her, although you could hardly complain if I did—damn it, Jen, I'm only human and you've got me on a very short leash right now!'

'It's good for you,' she told him shortly. 'Character-building. I've managed to abstain since the day you walked out. A few weeks won't do you any harm at all—and if I hear so much as a whisper about you and another woman, that's it. Savvy?'

He sighed. 'I savvy. You won't. That was weeks ago, anyway, and it's only you I really want. Look, are you sure that you can't come away this weekend? Mum and Dad would love to see you gain, and it would be wonderful to have some time together away from all this.'

It sounded all too cosy — as cosy as the jaws of a trap closing steadily around her. She shook her head.

'I can't — anyway, I'm working. They're short on Paeds.'

Nick's eyes narrowed sharply. 'Is Barrett on?'

Jennifer glared at him. 'Don't you dare get theatrical on me after you've been messing about with that Slater woman —— '

'Oh, God, we're back to that, are we?'

She closed her eyes. 'You really can't see it, can you? That old familiar double standard.'

'I'm sorry.'

And he sounded genuinely contrite, so she forgave him, and packed Tim off with a serious and chastened Nick. She spent the following morning rushing round doing the week's chores before changing back into her uniform and making her way to the hospital.

It took her all of ten minutes to get back into the swing.

Andrew was around, moving silently through the periphery of her schedule, appearing occasionally to ask how it was going.

Lucy Banks was her main concern. She was weak but seemed fairly stable, although Jennifer didn't like the hectic colour in her cheeks.

She perched on the bed and smiled. 'Haven't seen you downstairs recently — I gather you've moved in here almost permanently! How are you feeling?'

'Bored,' Lucy replied with a weak grin. 'I wish I

could do something, but I feel so tired I can't be bothered.'

Jennifer checked her obs, and noted her temperature was up a little. She mentioned it to Andrew, who decided to add another antibiotic to the cocktail.

The other girl she knew, Suzanne Hooper, was sullen but resigned. She had been taken off her drip that morning and was picking at her lunch when Jennifer went and sat in the dayroom next to her. All the others had gone and she was alone, chasing the food disconsolately round the plate.

'Do I have to eat all this?' she asked Jennifer despairingly.

'There isn't all that much. Please do your best, otherwise you'll have to have the drip back up.'

'Ugh. Oh, all right.' She chewed and swallowed with a certain amount of theatre, and Jennifer hid a smile. 'There isn't anything to do here. They're all just kids,' she went on.

'Not all. There are a few girls of your age — like Lucy, in the single room next to you. Why don't you go and talk to her?'

'What's wrong with her?'

'She's got a chest infection.'

'Oh. Well, I suppose I could. Can I leave that bit?'

Jennifer nodded and smiled her understanding. 'Well done.'

'Didn't really have a choice, did I?' Suzanne said ungraciously, and, pushing back her chair, she went off down the corridor towards the four-bedded bay she shared with one other girl.

Later that afternoon Jennifer noticed her sitting on

Lucy's bed, and they seemed to be getting on all right so she left them to it.

At six-thirty there was a lull, and Andrew called into the office.

'How about a quick bite to eat?'

She smiled at him. 'I haven't had a better offer all day! All this running about has made me starving!'

He grinned. 'Come on, then, before something happens.'

'Now what on earth could happen?'

'Don't!' he said fervently.

She laughed and stood up, unpinning her keys and giving them to the staff nurse on her way out.

As they ate, Andrew asked her how she had enjoyed her day.

'Busy, fun — I've missed nursing, but I had to do something that fitted in round Tim, and Outpatients is perfect.'

'You still nurse, you know.'

She shook her head. 'It's not the same.'

He fell silent for a moment, then asked, 'Did Tim get away all right?'

She nodded. 'I had a word with Nick, by the way. Seems it was just what you said, but he tried to imply it was my fault.'

Andrew's brows plucked together. 'Your fault?'

'Because I won't let him sleep with me ——'

Andrew choked on his coffee, and set the cup down with a smack in the saucer.

'What?' he spluttered.

She stared at him. 'What do you mean, what?'

Andrew flushed and looked away, then looked back. 'I just thought — I assumed. . .'

'So did Nick, but he was wrong.' She lifted her shoulders. 'I didn't want him to have an unfair advantage — after all, I hadn't slept with you. . .'

Andrew's bemused eyes searched her face, and then he sighed. 'No — no, you hadn't.' He looked down at his hands. 'I just took it for granted that by now you were — well, back to where you left off, if you like.'

She laughed softly. 'Oh, no, I think we're a little further on, actually. He's finding it very difficult — asking Nick to communicate with a woman without using sex is like cutting off an Italian's hands — it almost turns him into a deaf mute — but he's trying, and I don't know, maybe. . . Maybe this time it will work. Who knows?'

'Who indeed?' Andrew murmured thoughtfully. He stood up abruptly. 'Come on, we'd better go back up.'

They made their way back to the ward in a wary silence, and were greeted at the door by a flustered staff nurse.

'Oh, Sister, Dr Barrett, I'm glad you're back. I was just going to get them to page you. It's Lucy Banks. She's going downhill fast.'

Andrew and Jennifer moved smoothly into action, but there was nothing to be done.

At a quarter past eight, Lucy slipped quietly away.

Andrew was wonderful with her parents, and while he took them into the office Jennifer stayed with Lucy and dismantled the drip and oxygen mask and so on. While she was busy, she suddenly felt the hairs on the back of her neck prickle and she turned round.

Suzanne Hooper was standing there, her eyes like saucers in her white face.

'What happened?' she whispered.

'She died,' Jennifer replied gently. 'It was inevitable — she had cystic fibrosis, and a severe chest infection is often fatal.'

Suzanne moved forwards and touched Lucy's hand. 'It's still warm — I was talking to her earlier. She can't be dead!'

She looked up and met Jennifer's eyes. 'Oh, God, I never asked about her. She asked what was wrong with me, and I went on and on about how I had diabetes and it was awful and you might as well pass a death sentence on me, and now——'

She clapped a hand over her mouth and ran out of the cubicle. Jennifer stuck her head round and called a nearby nurse.

'Can you come and relieve me here? I must go after Suzanne.'

She turned back to Lucy and smoothed her hair back from her damp forehead, then stood for a moment holding the limp little hand before turning away.

'Will you be all right?' she asked the nurse, a first-year who looked nearly as shocked and upset as Suzanne.

She nodded, and Jennifer left her, almost running down the ward in Suzanne's footsteps.

She found her in the corner of the tinies' play room in the dark, curled up on a bean bag, crying her eyes out.

Jennifer didn't try to talk to her, but simply held her and let her cry.

'I thought I had problems,' she mumbled eventually, and Jennifer silently agreed.

Life — and death — had a way of putting one's troubles into perspective. When Suzanne was quiet,

Jennifer talked to her about Lucy and her illness and the effect it had had on her life, so that in the end she saw that it was almost a blessed release. By the time she finished, Suzanne was much calmer although still upset, and they went back to the ward together.

After a while she found Andrew, who had stayed with Mr and Mrs Banks for some time. He was far less philosophical.

'She was on the transplant register,' he raged quietly. 'Damn it, she shouldn't have died! Surely somewhere there must have been a suitable donor?'

She handed him a cup of coffee. 'God moves in mysterious ways,' she said.

'Doesn't He just,' Andrew said bitterly.

'Suzanne came in.'

He looked up at her, and closed his eyes. 'Oh, lord.'

'It may just have brought her to her senses.'

'Or pushed her over the brink.'

Jennifer shook her head. 'Somehow I don't think so. I'll get the night staff to keep an eye on her. Has anyone called the mortuary?'

'I did. They've been, and her parents have gone down with her to see her again. I'll go and talk to them. Are you in tomorrow?'

She nodded. 'I'll see you then.'

He eyed her keenly. 'Are you OK?'

'Yes, I think so.'

'I'm sorry it had to happen when you were on the ward.'

She smiled faintly. 'All part of life's rich pattern. That's why I went in to nursing. It won't do me any harm to be on the sharp end for a bit.'

Shortly afterwards she handed over, and then made her way home.

The flat seemed strangely lonely. For all the sadness, the ward with all its bustle seemed suddenly a much better place to be.

CHAPTER EIGHT

JENNIFER arrived on the ward in the morning to find Suzanne Hooper quietly eating her breakfast—all of it, without complaint.

Afterwards she went and lay on her bed, her eyes fixed on the door of Lucy's room. Jennifer approached her warily.

'Hi. Are you OK?'

She looked up, and Jennifer thought how empty her eyes were.

'I'm fine—I'll live, won't I? Unlike Lucy.'

Jennifer perched on the edge of the bed. 'Lucy had a viral infection—there was nothing we could do to help her. She was already so weakened that she couldn't fight it.'

'And all I could talk about was myself,' Suzanne said in a little voice.

Jennifer squeezed her hand. 'I don't suppose Lucy minded. I think she was probably sick of people asking her how she was.'

Suzanne met her eyes. 'I'm going to eat sensibly now. There are more important things in life than being thin—like being alive. I mean, diabetes is nothing really, is it?'

'Oh, I don't know. It still takes courage to deal with it, and it does place restrictions on you that can be irksome, but if you look after yourself there's no reason why you shouldn't lead a perfectly normal life.'

142

'It won't kill me, anyway. When Lucy died — if you could have seen her mother's eyes. . .'

She turned away, burying her face in the pillow, and Jennifer patted her shoulder and left her to it.

She wasn't surprised to see Andrew already on the ward shortly after nine. There had been an emergency admission, a child with a tummy bug who was so dehydrated his skin was like crêpe paper.

Andrew put him on a drip of normal saline and glucose, and gradually he started to pick up during the course of the morning.

They found time for a quick cup of coffee late in the morning in the ward office, and Andrew slumped in the chair opposite Jennifer and rolled his head on his shoulders.

'Bad night?' she said softly.

'Like you wouldn't believe,' he groaned. 'Two kids in ITU, one with burns and smoke inhalation after a fireworks party that went wrong, and one in status asthmaticus.'

'Are they OK?'

'I think they will be, but it was a long old night.' He drained his coffee and stood up. 'You were right about Suzanne, by the way. As you said, God moves in mysterious ways. I must get on. I'll be in ITU if you need me.'

She watched him go, his broad frame filling the doorway briefly before he was gone from view, his quiet footsteps fading away very quickly.

The room seemed empty without him.

She went down to the canteen for lunch at one and found the sort of quiet buzz that accompanied bad news.

Kathleen Hennessy and Jack Lawrence from A and E were sitting with Mary O'Brien, the orthopaedics sister, and they all looked shocked. Jennifer joined them.

'What's happened?' she asked curiously.

'Clare and Michael are missing,' Kathleen said quietly. 'Someone picked up a Mayday, and the air-sea rescue helicopters have found the boat empty. There's no sign of them, but the dinghy's missing too, so they're hoping they might pick them up in it, but the weather off the Scillies is foul, apparently, and God alone knows how long they'll survive in this cold.'

Jennifer felt the shock right through to her toes. 'When did it happen?'

'Early this morning,' Mary told her. 'About four or thereabouts. It was Clare's voice, apparently.'

'I wonder what happened?' she murmured.

'Lord knows,' Mary said. 'I'm going up to the chapel for a minute. Are you coming?'

Kathleen nodded. 'I won't be long,' she said to Jack, and he squeezed her hand.

'You go and say your Hail Marys for them. God knows it can't do any harm.'

'You're an old cynic, do you know that?' Mary scolded him fondly.

He grinned briefly. 'Less of the old.'

Jennifer watched them go, then turned to Jack. 'You're the expert — how long have they got in an open boat?'

He shrugged. 'Depends — on the wind, how wet they are, what they're wearing, if they've got anything to eat, when they had their last meal — all sorts of things.'

'Just answer the question,' she pushed gently.

He pursed his lips. 'Anything from one to twelve hours—maybe longer if all the conditions are right, and always assuming they're in the boat. If they've got flares they should be able to attract attention, but the Atlantic's awfully big.'

Jennifer sighed. 'It's the third thing.'

Jack's brows twitched together in a puzzled frown.

'First Michael's leg, then Clare's ectopic, now this.'

'Are you superstitious?'

She gave a hollow laugh. 'Only when something like this happens.'

They shared a smile.

'Your ex is covering for Michael, isn't he?'

'Word travels,' she said drily.

'Of course—this is a hospital, Jennifer!'

'Well, so it is—I'd forgotten!' she joked, and then they fell silent again, both preoccupied.

Jack leant back in his chair, cradling his coffee-cup. 'I rather thought you and Barrett were an item, but then the jungle drums said something about you and Nick getting back together.'

'Why are hospital staff so damn nosy?'

Jack laughed and apologised. 'After proposing to Kathleen in front of the entire nation on live television, I tend to forget people like their privacy.'

She chuckled. 'That was a priceless bit of theatre— your face when you saw the camera was comical!'

He grinned. 'Yes, well—let's just say it slipped out in an unguarded moment.'

'So when's the big day?'

'Just after Christmas—we're going over to Ireland. I have to meet the family next weekend. I can't say I'm looking forward to it.'

'They'll love you—you're marrying their precious girl, after all. Her mother's been after Kathleen to get married for years!'

His face fell. 'Yes, well, I'm not an ideal choice. I'm too old, I can't have children—far from perfect for a good Catholic girl.'

'Kathleen looks pretty happy to me.'

He gave a twisted grin. 'She is. She's managed to convince me—now she just has to convince her mother that she really doesn't need any more grandchildren, because there's no way we'd risk having a child with CF.'

'You lost a son to it, didn't you?'

'Jungle drums again?'

She smiled apologetically. 'Word gets around. We run the CF clinic, of course, so it's fairly relevant to us in a way.'

'You lost a girl last night with CF, didn't you?'

She nodded again. 'Yes—Lucy. Lovely girl. It's such a waste.'

'It always is,' he said quietly, and with a heavy sigh he unfolded his long legs and stood up. 'Sorry to abandon you, but I have to get back.'

She watched him go, and thought again how fortunate she was that Tim had been born healthy. Maybe she should just bite the bullet and say yes to Nick, and then work on their relationship. After all, it couldn't be that bad, could it?

Nick returned Tim at six that evening—a Tim who was quite clearly bubbling over with excitement and yet clearly edgy about something.

'I gather the Barringtons are missing — it's on the radio,' Nick said.

'Yes.' She answered absently, her eyes on Tim. 'Yes, they are, it's awful. Tim, what's wrong?'

'Oh, it's the kitten. He's worried you'll be mad with him, but I've told him I'll talk you round.'

'Kitten?' Her eyes swivelled back to Nick, appalled. 'What kitten?'

Nick shrugged helplessly. 'We went to my parents' neighbours last night for a bonfire party, and they had some Burmese kittens just ready to go — there was one still available, and Tim just fell in love with the little chap.'

Jennifer could hardly believe her ears. 'Are you quite mad? What are you thinking about, Nick? He can't have a kitten here!'

'He's trained to use a litter tray — really, he'd be no trouble — '

'Nick, we aren't allowed pets here.'

'Not even one little kitten?'

She sighed. 'No. Not even a damn goldfish! It'll have to go back.'

'But I can't take it back! I've bought it now — '

'Well, you should have thought of that before. I can't have it here.'

Nick eyed Tim thoughtfully. 'Did you know you weren't allowed pets here?'

Tim squirmed uncomfortably and avoided his eye. 'You did say we might be moving soon, Mum,' he mumbled.

Nick's eyes flew back to Jennifer's. 'Really?'

'That was — before,' she said evasively, but Nick understood the implication.

His mouth hardened. 'Well, he'll have to come here for the night and we'll sort something out tomorrow. I'll bring the stuff in.'

He went out, and Jennifer turned to Tim.

'Really, Tim, you've gone too far this time.'

He stuck his chin out mulishly. 'But I wanted a kitten — I've wanted one for ages —— '

'And you knew you couldn't have one. You were very naughty to persuade your father to get you one. I think you'd better go to your room.'

'Perhaps Andrew can have him?' he said hopefully.

'Andrew's got more than enough cats. Now scoot.'

'But Mum —— '

'No. Go on, I'll talk to you later. I'm very cross.'

Nick reappeared just as Tim slammed his door. 'Oh, dear. I'm sorry, darling, I didn't realise —— '

'Well, if you'd given it any thought at all instead of acting on impulse as usual, you would have at least rung to ask me.'

'I tried, but you were out, remember?'

She sighed. 'Yes, I was. Even so —— '

'I shouldn't have done it. I'm sorry. Anyway, here he is.'

Nick handed her a cardboard pet carrier, and she opened the top and peeped in.

'Oh, he's sweet! How old is he?'

'Ten weeks.'

She reached in and lifted out the little bundle of fluff and eyes. The kitten miaowed pathetically, and she smoothed his fur with a gentle finger and put him down. He immediately relieved himself on the carpet.

'Litter trained, you said?'

'Oh, hell!' Nick crouched beside her and glared at

the unrepentant kitten, who sniffed his offering and then sauntered off across the living-room, checking out his surroundings.

'Make yourself at home,' she said drily to the little cat, and he miaowed at her, climbed into her slipper and fell instantly asleep.

She glanced at Nick. 'You can clear that up.'

'Oh, no!'

She smirked. 'Oh, yes. I'll make you a cup of coffee, and then you can go.'

She was in the kitchen when Nick called.

'Has the boyfriend got one of those Japanese Tonka-toys?'

She poked her head out of the kitchen. 'If by that you mean an Isuzu Trooper, then yes,' she said drily. 'Why?'

'Because he's just pulled up outside.'

'Really?' She glanced out of the window. Sure enough, Andrew was just climbing out of the car.

'Maybe he'll know someone who wants the cat,' she said thoughtfully.

'Tim wants the cat.'

'Well, Tim can't have the blasted cat. Have you cleared that mess up yet?'

'Nag, nag, nag,' Nick mumbled, but retreated into the bathroom with a handful of soiled tissues.

Seconds later the bell rang, and she went to the door. Andrew's bulky frame filled the doorway.

'Come in — can I get you a coffee?'

'Have you got time?'

'We were just about to have one.'

'We?' He hesitated on the threshold.

'Nick's here — come in, Andrew.'

He shook his head. 'No, I won't stop. I'm sorry, I didn't realise Nick was here. I just wanted to tell you the news — Clare and Michael have been picked up. They've got hypothermia, and Michael's got a cut on his eyebrow, but they're alive.'

She sagged against the wall. 'Oh, thank God.'

She turned to Nick as he emerged from the bathroom drying his hands. 'The Barringtons have been found — they're alive.'

Nick gave a wry laugh. 'Bang goes my permanent job.'

Jennifer was horrified. 'For God's sake! They're friends of mine — do you know what you're implying?'

'Oh, lord,' he groaned. 'I'm sorry, that was a tasteless remark.'

'Oh, you noticed,' she said angrily.

'Jen, I've said I'm sorry — I didn't realise they were friends. Of course I didn't want anything to happen to them. Damn it, I'd be a fine doctor if I wanted people to die, wouldn't I?'

'I've given up trying to fathom how your mind works,' she muttered under her breath, and, grabbing Andrew's arm, she dragged him into the room.

'You have to help me,' she told him. 'I have a problem. This idiot and his son have produced a kitten — I can't keep it here. I wondered if you knew of someone who would give it a home.'

Andrew closed his eyes. 'Oh, Jennifer, no!' he moaned. 'Not another cat!'

'Oh, not you! I wouldn't dream of asking you to take him.'

He opened his eyes and searched her face. 'Where is he?'

She pointed to her slipper, and a smile tiptoed over his face. He crouched down beside it and stroked the kitten's ears. It peered up at him out of huge blue-green eyes.

'What a rascal.'

'The rascal,' she informed him drily, 'has already christened the carpet.'

'Oh.'

'Yes, oh,' Nick said. 'And guess who had to clear it up?'

Andrew chuckled. 'Character-building. Is he Burmese?'

Nick nodded. 'Yes. He's got a magnificent pedigree.'

'I'm sure,' Andrew said drily. 'He'll still claw the furniture and steal food off the worktops. Oh, little fellow, you're gorgeous.'

His big hand cupped the tiny kitten and scooped him out of the slipper. Immediately a loud purr poured out of the tiny body, and he snuggled closer to Andrew's chest.

Andrew straightened. 'Is he hungry?'

Jennifer lifted her shoulders in despair. 'I have no idea.'

Andrew chuckled. 'I can see you're really into this.'

Her shoulders drooped. 'Oh, Andrew, I love cats, but we can't keep him here, and now we've got him Tim is going to be so difficult!'

Andrew glanced from Jennifer to Nick and back again.

'Why don't I look after him for you — just for now? Then — later, we can make other plans.'

She looked up into his face, and read there all the uncertainty that she was feeling over their future.

Would it be with Nick, or him?

At the moment it was hard to choose. She knew, if she was honest, that it was Andrew she wanted to be with, but she didn't think he loved her. And if she was settling for a tepid relationship built on fondness rather than the white heat of passion, then shouldn't it be with her son's father?

Whatever, it didn't solve the immediate problem of the kitten.

'Could you?' she said hesitantly. 'And then, later. . .'

He nodded understandingly. 'Sure. Don't worry, I'll look after him for you.'

'What about Blu-Tack?'

His mouth lifted in a wry grin. 'Blu-Tack will cope. Does this horror have a name?'

'Cadbury.'

They both glanced at Nick in surprise. 'Cadbury?'

Nick lifted his shoulders. 'It's the colour.'

Andrew smoothed the brown coat with his finger. 'OK, Cadbury, let's take you home.'

Jennifer glanced at the kitten, curled up on Andrew's big, warm hand, and thought she must have gone mad. Fancy being jealous of a kitten!

After a few days in hospital, the Barringtons returned to *Henrietta* moored in the Scilly Isles, and sailed her back to Shotley in Suffolk.

They returned to the hospital a week later to be greeted with a hero's welcome. Apart from a small stitched cut over Michael's left eyebrow which simply added to his devastating good looks, they appeared perfectly well and happy.

The next evening at her flat, Nick told Jennifer that Michael had been following him round, 'Almost checking up on me! Damn cheek!'

'And what did he find?'

Nick grinned disarmingly. 'Actually, he said hard as he tried he couldn't find any fault!'

Jennifer chuckled. 'I expect he was just being nice.'

'No faith in me, have you?'

She smiled. 'Should I have?'

Nick sobered. 'I wish you did. I love you, Jen. I wish I could be sure it was enough.'

She looked away.

'Jen? I've only got ten days left now. Am I getting anywhere?'

His voice was soft, coaxing, and she could feel herself weakening. It would be so easy. . .

His bleep shattered the quiet, and he swore under his breath and silenced it. 'I must go.' He stood up and pulled her into her arms, hugging her. 'Just remember I love you.'

His kiss was gentle and undemanding, and then he was gone, leaving her even more confused.

Suzanne Hooper came in to the diabetic clinic on Tuesday and was much better. For the first time her blood sugar was in the normal range, and she told them she'd been eating properly and had stopped making herself sick.

'It was silly, really. I looked at some photos of me taken in the summer, and I looked scrawny and awful. I didn't realise I'd lost so much weight till I saw them.'

She had regained a little of the lost weight since her stay in hospital, her cheeks were filling out and she looked ten times better than she had.

The clinical psychologist was delighted with her and didn't want to see her again unless she or Andrew felt it was necessary, and her mother was over the moon.

She had even apparently been to Lucy Banks's funeral, and had formed a tentative relationship with Lucy's parents.

After she went out, Andrew commented on that to Jennifer.

'I spoke to Mrs Banks a couple of days ago, and she told me Suzanne had been in touch. Said what a comfort it was to know that Lucy's death had helped Suzanne to make sense of her own life. She said it made it seem less of a waste.'

'How are they coping?'

'Oh, so-so. It's hard.'

'It must be. I keep looking at Tim and wondering how it would feel to lose him.'

'Don't. Talking of Tim, do you want to come out at the weekend and see Cadbury?'

'Oh, Tim'd love to. How is the little rotter?'

Andrew chuckled. 'Awful. He's so naughty—he's highly intelligent, and so quick—he's everywhere. I lost him last night, and eventually found him in my bed. God knows how he got up there—must have climbed up the side of the quilt, because he can't jump that high yet.'

'I expect he just wanted a bit of peace and quiet—it must be fairly chaotic with seven cats.'

'Don't remind me,' he said with a groan. 'I'm on

call, but I can pick you up any time — just tell me when.'

Her heart sank as she remembered something — something she really shouldn't have forgotten.

'Look, can we leave it a week?' she asked tiredly. 'It's Nick's last weekend, and I think he wants to spend it with us.'

Andrew nodded. She thought she saw a flicker of disappointment in his eyes, but there was no way she would stake her life on it. Probably just wishful thinking. 'That'll be better, really. The weekends tend to get a little hectic.'

'I noticed,' she told him wryly. 'Right, shall I wheel in the next?'

The weekend was cold but bright, as only late November days could be, and they drove up to Norfolk and went for a walk along the cliffs at Cromer on Saturday. Nick suggested staying in a hotel, but when Jennifer pointed out that she would be sleeping with Tim he gave her a resigned smile and drove them home.

On Sunday they went to the zoo, and Tim announced that he thought zoos were cruel and animals should be left to roam free in the wild.

Nevertheless he seemed to enjoy seeing them, and they had a lovely day which ended with a meal cooked for them at the flat by Nick.

He managed to avoid all the things Tim hated, and Jennifer thought how much he'd changed.

He seemed to be making a real effort now, and she realised with surprise that she would miss him when he went away.

Although she wasn't convinced that she loved him,

he was what he had never been before, a friend, and she found she treasured that new relationship.

She told him so after Tim had gone to bed, and his eyes brightened with hope.

'You don't have to miss me, you know. You could always come back to me.'

She stared at him, unable to answer for a moment, and he took her hand, staring down at it and turning her wedding-ring on her finger.

'Come away with me for the weekend. Just us, on our own. Have a week or two after I'm gone, to let the dust settle, and then maybe when you've forgotten all my irritating little habits I'll be able to talk you into it.' He tipped her chin up so that she had to meet his eyes, and she could see the passion blazing in them.

'We used to be good together, Jen. Give us a chance.'

Swallowing hard, she nodded. 'OK. I'll come for the weekend—not this one coming, the next. Two weeks from now.'

He studied her gravely for a moment. 'How many rooms do I book?'

She took a deep breath, then leapt into the abyss. 'One.'

The smile slowly lit his eyes, and he hugged her gently. 'Thank you. I'd better go, it's late and I might forget my good intentions.'

He pulled her up and kissed her, and then hugged her again before heading for the door.

She stopped him just before he left. 'Nick?'

'Yes?'

'It doesn't necessarily mean I'm coming back to you.'

After a second he nodded. 'OK.' He winked. 'I'll have to make sure I surpass myself.'

She tried to answer his smile, and then the door closed and he was gone, and she was left wondering what on earth she'd done.

CHAPTER NINE

AFTER Nick went, the evening seemed long and empty. Jennifer sat with Tim and did his homework, and then after his bath they curled up on the settee in front of the television and chatted before he had to go to bed.

On the Friday evening Tim was allowed to stay up a little later, and he snuggled up to Jennifer's side and rested his head on her shoulder. After a while she thought he had gone to sleep, but then he spoke, his voice very quiet, so she had to strain to hear him.

'Are you going back to live with him again?'

She tilted her head round and looked down at him. 'I'm not sure,' she said honestly. 'How would you feel about it.'

He thought for a moment, then shrugged his little shoulders. 'Dunno. He's much nicer now than he was — he doesn't make me eat chips and he listens — do you know what I mean?'

'Yes, I do. He listens to me now, too.'

Tim sighed. 'I wonder how Cadbury is.'

'We're going to see him tomorrow,' Jennifer told him, and was rewarded with a brilliant smile.

'Really? Great! When?'

'We're going over for lunch — Andrew's going to pick us up at twelve and bring us back later.'

'Magic! I'll be able to feed the chickens and play with all the kittens — are my jeans clean?'

She smiled indulgently. 'I think they're clean now, but I don't know how long for.'

He laughed and hugged her. 'It's ages since we've been there. I can't wait. I'm going to go to bed now so there isn't so much time. It goes quicker when you're asleep.'

It seemed like a good idea, but unfortunately it didn't work so well for adults, clearly, as it did for children — especially not adults who were torn between anticipation and dread. After all, it was probably going to be the last time she was with him away from work, and it would doubtless be a day of very mixed feelings. She felt a twinge of anxiety because Tim seemed so much more enthusiastic about a weekend with Andrew than a lifetime with Nick, but she told herself it was early days, and their love for each other would grow. She didn't dare to dwell too long on the thought that she, too, was looking forward more to tomorrow than to the following weekend. After all, there were Andrew's feelings to consider too, and by now she was quite certain that he didn't love her, or at least not in that way.

He arrived promptly at twelve, and they were downstairs waiting. Tim flew across the car park and threw himself into Andrew's arms, and when Andrew set him down his eyes were full of emotion.

He looked up at Jennifer and smiled warily. 'Hi.'

'Hi. We're all ready.'

'Good. Come on, then.'

Maybe it was the tension, or perhaps just because she had grown used to Nick, but Andrew seemed awfully big sitting beside her, and she found her eyes straying again and again to his large and capable hands on the wheel, and the shift of his powerful thighs every time he changed gear.

In fact she was so tinglingly aware of him that it was almost a relief when they arrived and she was able to escape the confines of the car.

'Where's Cadbury?' Tim asked excitedly, and Andrew opened the door and led them into the kitchen.

The kitten had grown enormously, and seemed all ears and eyes and long legs. He was extremely vocal, showing his oriental breeding, and Tim was absolutely captivated.

Jennifer helped Andrew prepare a simple meal for lunch, which kept her hands busy and her mind slightly occupied. However, every time she caught his eye, she knew they were going to have to talk soon, and she found her appetite deserted her.

As it was a warm day for early December, Tim took all the kittens outside after lunch and played with them on the lawn, while Jennifer and Andrew sat inside and watched through the windows. She pretended absorption with their antics, but she wasn't fooling either Andrew or herself.

His voice was soft, slightly rough.

'Jennifer?'

The expression in his eyes arrested her. She had never seen such emptiness before. With resignation, she realised it was time to talk.

'Are you OK?' she asked him hesitantly.

His mouth twisted in a wry smile. 'I'll do. How about you? You must be missing Nick,' he said quietly, in the same soft, scrapy voice.

She nodded thoughtfully. 'It's funny, I never thought

I would, but in a way it's awfully quiet without him. He's changed — grown up, I suppose.'

Andrew straightened away from the window-sill and turned his attention to the fire, poking it half-heartedly.

'So, what happens now?' he asked eventually.

She drew a deep breath. 'He's asked me to go away with him for the weekend.'

His shoulders stiffened slightly. 'And?'

'I've said I'll go.'

'You're going back to him,' he said flatly.

'I — probably. I think so.' It depends, she wanted to say, on whether you want me still, but the words stayed locked in her throat.

She stared at his back, willing him to turn round and say he loved her, but he didn't. He stayed crouched by the fire, his back to her, and eventually he sighed and straightened up, and his words sent her last glimmer of hope crashing into the dust.

'I think you're doing the right thing. He loves you — Tim's his son. It makes sense, really. . .'

He threw a log on the fire, and when he turned to face her his expression was carefully blank. His voice, however, had a slight rasp that could have been the smoke, or there again. . .

'I'll miss you both,' he said huskily.

'Don't!' she choked, and then somehow she was in his arms, burying her face against his solid chest and cursing the tears that spilled over and scalded her cheeks.

'Don't cry,' he pleaded, and smoothed her hair with his warm, heavy hand. It made it worse, to be so tenderly cradled in his arms for what must be the last

time, and she dragged herself away and blotted her
cheeks on a ragged tissue she found in her pocket.

'I'm sorry—this is ridiculous. I ought to be happy,
but—I'm going to miss you, too.'

The tears started again, and he sat down and tugged
her on to his lap and let her get on with it. Eventually
she pulled herself together and sat up, sniffing.

'I'm sorry,' she mumbled, 'but it's been so difficult,
and you've been so kind about it, and I can't bear to
hurt you——'

'Don't worry about me, I'm fine. I just want you to
be happy, and if Nick's the man to do that, then so be
it. Now dry your eyes and let's go and see what Tim's
up to before the kittens freeze to death.'

So that was that. He was fine, he'd said so, and she
might as well go to Nick. He, at least, loved her.

Andrew took them home soon after that, in a silence
fraught with emotion, and that night she cried herself
to sleep.

Nick rang the next day, and Tim chatted happily to
him for a while before handing her the phone.

'He wants to talk to you.'

They discussed the plans for the weekend, and then
she hung up, to find Tim watching her thoughtfully.

'Are we going away somewhere?'

'I am, with your father. You're going to stay with
Anne.'

'Oh,' he said, and that was all. It was rather how she
felt herself.

It was a difficult week. Andrew was busy, and he
looked more tired and strained than she had ever seen
him. As the weekend drew nearer, so her nerves were

strung tighter than a bowstring and she became inefficient and tearful.

Then, at lunchtime on Friday, Anne rang to say that her son had had a fall at school and broken his arm, and she was unable to have Tim for the weekend.

After all the build-up and anticipation, nerving herself up for what was bound to be an emotionally traumatic reunion that she was at best half-hearted about, the thought of having to go through the same process all over again was too much to take.

She went into the department's little kitchen, shut the door and burst into tears, astonishing Beattie who was making a cup of tea for everyone.

'Oh, my love, whatever's happened?' she asked, and wrapped a motherly arm around Jennifer's shoulders.

'I just wanted it to be over,' she sobbed, and Beattie, with all the instinct of a mother hen, hugged and patted and soothed, which just made it worse.

Then Andrew's deep rumble sounded near her ear, and Beattie's yielding bosom gave way to Andrew's solid chest, and the tears fell even faster.

'Oh, love, don't cry,' Andrew murmured, his large hand cradling her head against his heart, and gradually the steady beat soothed her and the tears slowed.

'Do you want to tell me?'

She sniffed and found a large white handkerchief in her hand. She scrubbed her cheeks, blew her nose and shoved her bedraggled hair back off her face.

'My childminder rang. She can't have Tim for the weekend, and I haven't got anybody else, and it means I can't go away with Nick this weekend, and I don't think I can bear it if we have to put it off. . .'

Another sob rose in her throat, and she pressed the

handkerchief against her mouth and fought for some control. Andrew's hand fell away from her shoulder, and he turned away.

'I'll have Tim for you.'

Her eyes flew up and searched the stiff set of his shoulders for any clue, but there was none.

'I couldn't ask you to do that——'

'You haven't asked, I've offered. I'm not on call this weekend, so there's no problem. If I have to come in, he can always come with me. He can play with the kittens and help me in the garden—really, Jennifer. It's not a problem.'

He turned slowly, and his smile was strained. 'You go. We'll be fine.'

Her eyes locked with his, and deep in their amber depths she looked for the love she hoped to find, but there was nothing.

She nodded. 'If you're sure. . .'

'I'm sure. Now wash your face and slap on some war-paint and let's get on with the clinic.'

It was long and slow, the usual Friday afternoon mixed bag of children who were failing to thrive, who were too short or too heavy or too thin, or had tummy-ache for no reason, and children who had had treatment and were coming back for check-ups.

One of these was Gemma Edwards, the little girl with recurrent UTIs who had had surgery for her faulty bladder valves to correct her reflux.

She had had another micturating cystourethrogram, and the problem appeared to be solved.

She was as perky as ever, and Jennifer set her troubles aside and concentrated on her patient.

'I don't get sore wee-wees any more,' she told

Jennifer proudly. 'And my friends at school are all jealous 'cos I've been in hospital.'

'Are they, sweetheart? Well, there you are, then! Famous!'

Gemma giggled. 'I'm not 'zactly famous, but it was lots of fun. When we play Doctors and Nurses, I get to be the doctor now, 'cos I know all about it!'

Andrew smiled. 'Is that right? Well, when you're bigger you'll have to come back and do your training and be a proper doctor, won't you?'

He straightened her clothes and winked at her. 'Just for now, you concentrate on drinking lots of water and enjoying yourself, OK?'

'OK!' she chirped brightly, and hopped off the couch. 'Can we go now?'

Andrew nodded. 'Yes, I don't think I need to see you again, but keep an eye on it, Mrs Edwards, and go straight to your GP if you see any sign of trouble. I'll see Gemma again immediately, all right?'

Mrs Edwards nodded and shook his hand. 'Thank you so much, Dr Barrett. You've been wonderful.'

He flushed slightly and smiled. 'You're welcome. All part of the service.'

They left, and Jennifer felt her heart race.

'Is that it?' Andrew asked, and she nodded.

'Yes, that's it.'

Their eyes met. 'You'd better go and get ready, then. What time shall I pick Tim up?'

'We can run him over to you. I don't know what time Nick's arriving.'

'I'd rather fetch him. Shall we say six-thirty?'

She nodded. Of course he wouldn't want Nick coming to his house. She was suddenly assailed by doubts. How could she ask him to have Tim while she and Nick —— ?

Her throat closed, and she swallowed hard.

'Go on,' he said harshly, and turned away. 'I'll clear up here.'

'Right.'

She hovered for a second, then turned on her heel and almost ran out of the department and round the corner of the hospital to the flats where she and her childminder both lived. Anne's sister had come over to look after her other children and had picked Tim up from school, and she collected him, sent a message to Anne that she hoped James would soon be better and almost dragged Tim back to their flat.

'Does that mean you aren't going?' he asked hopefully, and she stopped, her key in the door, and looked at him.

'Why?'

He shrugged, suddenly uncommunicative. 'Nothing.'

'You're going to stay with Andrew instead.'

His face lit up. 'Really? All weekend?'

She stared at his eager face with misgiving. Was she doing the right thing? She hadn't wanted them to get too close, but they seemed to have such a natural affinity for each other. . .

'All weekend.'

'Magic!'

He almost shrieked the word, and was positively bouncing on the spot.

'Come on, wretch,' she said fondly, hiding her doubts, and sent him off to his room to pack the last-minute things. Then she had a quick bath and washed her hair, hanging over the bed as usual to dry it.

She had almost finished when the doorbell rang.

It was only twenty past six, and she sent Tim to get it, confident that it would be Nick.

But it wasn't, it was Andrew, and they stood one each side of the sitting-room, their eyes locked.

She was in her underwear with a dressing-gown pulled hastily over the top, and she was desperately conscious of her flushed cheeks and the wild tangle of her hair. So, evidently, was Andrew.

'I'll get dressed,' she said breathlessly, and ran back into her room, pulling on the forest-green jersey dress she had chosen to wear for travelling.

With her shoes on and her hair quickly brushed, she felt a little less vulnerable, and when she went back out Andrew was standing by the window, his expression carefully schooled.

'Get your things, Tim,' she instructed in a slightly shaky voice, and Tim instantly disappeared.

His voice came back out of his room. 'Have you seen that book, Mum? The library book about fungi?'

'It's in your bookcase.'

She met Andrew's eyes, and they were under control again.

'It's awfully good of you to have him.'

'It's a pleasure. You know what I think of him.'

'Yes.'

Then there was nothing more to say—at least, nothing that could be said, and she closed her eyes and turned away.

'Tim? Come on, darling. Andrew's waiting,' she called desperately.

He emerged from his room carrying a small case and a huge book.

'Got everything?' Andrew asked, his voice a little gruff, and Tim nodded.

'Let's go, then.'

Tim flung his arms around Jennifer and hugged her tight, and she kissed the top of his head and hugged him back hard.

'Off you go, then. Daddy and I will pick you up on Sunday afternoon.'

She looked up at Andrew. 'I'll ring you.'

He nodded curtly, then turned as he reached the door.

For a long moment their eyes met, then he swung the door open and ushered Tim out, just as Nick arrived. Jennifer's heart sank. She really hadn't wanted this to happen!

Nick's eyes swept over the scene, and one brow arched. 'Abducting my son?' he joked.

Tim filled the pause. 'Hi, Dad. I'm spending the weekend with Andrew because James has broken his arm and Anne can't have me.'

Nick looked slightly bemused. 'If you say so,' he murmured, and met Andrew's eyes. 'This is very generous of you.'

Andrew's mouth curled in a bitter smile. 'Anything to help Jennifer — anyway, Tim and I are good friends, aren't we, sport?'

Tim nodded. 'You should see Cadbury, Dad — he's into everything, and he talks all the time.'

'Sounds like a child,' Nick murmured.

'Well, he is a child,' Tim said reasonably, and Nick laughed a little tightly.

'So he is. Well, you be good, now. We'll see you on Sunday.'

'One thing,' Andrew said quietly, and Jennifer wondered if she had imagined the thread of steel in his voice. 'Take care of her.'

Nick returned Andrew's challenging stare with a victor's smile. 'I will.'

Then they were gone, their footsteps retreating down the stairs, and she was alone with Nick.

'All ready?'

'I just want to put on some make-up.'

She disappeared into the bathroom, her hands shaking, and took longer than was either necessary or probable to do her face.

Finally, unable to stall any longer, she went back into the sitting-room.

Nick was sitting on the arm of the settee, one leg dangling, and he eyed her thoughtfully. 'Was it wise, letting Andrew take him?'

'I had no other choice at such short notice. Why? Don't you trust him?'

He straightened up, shrugging slightly. 'It's not a case of trust. I just think it's rather hard on him to ask him to look after Tim while we go off together for the weekend.'

'I agree, but I didn't ask, he offered. Anyway, I don't think he cares that much ——'

Her voice cracked a little, and she went into her bedroom and closed her case.

'OK, let's go.'

The hotel was elegant and hushed, and in the quiet lobby Nick's voice seemed unnaturally loud.

'Mr and Mrs Davidson,' he told the receptionist, and

her heart tripped. It was so long since they had been linked in that way that it sounded strange.

Their luggage was taken up for them, and they went straight into the bar and then in to the dining-room. Perhaps the avoidance of the room was coincidence, perhaps not. Whatever, it was a relief to Jennifer.

The surroundings were plush, the food superb, and the service attentive — so attentive that they were able to avoid any but the most trivial conversation during dinner. She realised with surprise with Nick, too, was nervous — possibly even more nervous than she was, and they had both taken refuge in the ritual of the meal, then the coffee, then the second cup.

Finally, however, there was nothing left to hide behind.

His mouth lifting in a parody of a smile, Nick made a slight gesture with his hand. 'Shall we?'

She nodded, her throat suddenly tight. Why was she so nervous? This was her husband, the man she had married nine years before. Nothing that happened tonight would be new or strange. Why, then, did she feel this terrifying sense of dread?

They travelled up in the lift in silence, and Nick opened the door courteously and ushered her in.

The bedroom was beautiful, decorated in soft pastels with low lighting, and there were flowers on the table — red roses, just about to open, but quite without scent.

A lump appeared in her throat. Andrew had given her roses, but they had been heavy with scent, their petals beaded with dew, less perfect perhaps but somehow more real.

But she wasn't with Andrew, she was with Nick, and she did love him — really, she did. He was a good

friend, and he was Tim's father. It would be all right.
She just hoped to God that all right would be enough.

Nick turned her towards him, and cupping her face
in his hands, he lowered his head and brushed her lips
gently.

'You're beautiful tonight,' he murmured, and his lips
caressed hers again. Then his arms slid round her and
drew her close, and his mouth claimed hers in a kiss
that should have rocked the world.

Oh, lord, I must feel something! she thought desperately. Maybe if I close my eyes and pretend it's
Andrew. . .

As the thought registered, a little whimper of distress
rose in her throat. Nick's arms fell away, and he
stepped back. In the silence that followed, the only
sound was his slightly ragged breathing. Her eyes
fluttered open. He was watching her, his brilliant blue
gaze dulled with defeat.

'Nick. . .?'

'I've lost you, haven't I?'

His voice was gravelly and low, heavy with resignation. She closed her eyes again, unable to look at
him. 'It's not that I don't love you — you'll always mean
a lot to me, but somehow ——'

'You don't belong to me any more. I'm not sure you
ever really did — not for years, at least. I don't think
it's just Andrew either, is it?'

She shook her head numbly.

'Look at me — I won't bite.'

She looked up then, and his tender smile made her
want to weep.

'That's better. Now, tell me. Is it because of
Andrew?'

She shook her head again. 'No. The timing was unfortunate because it just clouded the issue, or maybe it helped me to realise what I should feel, but — he doesn't return my love, so it's really academic. . .' Her voice cracked and she sat down heavily on the bed.

'Oh, Jen.' Nick sat beside her and laid an arm round her shoulders. 'I think you're wrong. I think he does love you.'

'But he's never said so.'

Nick sighed wearily. 'Perhaps because he's too much of a gentleman. I think he backed off because he felt if our marriage could work it should be given a chance. If it hadn't been for Tim I don't know that he would have been so philosophical.'

She tipped her head round and met his eyes, unable to trust the little flicker of hope inside her. 'Really? You think he loves me?'

Nick shrugged. 'He's never said so to me, but I got the impression — why don't you go to him? If he does love you, he'll be going through hell at the moment.'

She nodded. 'Perhaps tomorrow — I want time to think.'

'Jen, about Tim. . .'

His face was sad, and she squeezed his hand.

'You're Tim's father. You always will be. Nothing's going to change that. He needs you, Nick — and so do I, in a way. I hope we can stay friends, because I'd miss your friendship now if I lost it.' She hesitated, then went on, slowly, 'I'm sorry I can't be what you want me to be. I would, if I could, but I just can't.'

'It would be tidy, wouldn't it — almost too tidy. Nature isn't like that. You go to him.'

She looked into his cobalt eyes. 'With your blessing?'

He hesitated for an age, then his mouth twisted into a wry smile. 'Yes, with my blessing. I want you, Jen, but willingly, on equal terms — not like this, like a lamb to the slaughter. I'll miss you, make no mistake, but in a way I guess I owe Andrew. If it hadn't been for him, you might have come back to me and we could have wasted the next few years in a tepid relationship that would never have worked.'

'Do you think so?'

He nodded. 'Don't you?'

She smiled softly. 'Probably. Oh, Nick. . .'

His arms were warm and gentle, undemanding. She let herself enjoy the luxury of their comfort for a moment, then straightened.

There was one last thing. With a little twist, she pulled off her wedding-ring and handed it to him.

He swallowed hard, and slipped it into his pocket. 'Do you want me to take you home?'

She nodded. 'Would you?'

'Of course.'

She should have rung. There was no guarantee he would want to see her, especially not at three in the morning, but she couldn't stand the suspense.

The taxi had gone, leaving her standing on the drive, her breath frosting on the cold night air.

There was a light on upstairs — Tim's room, she realised — and another in the kitchen.

As she approached, her heart in her mouth, she heard the sweet strains of Fauré's *Requiem*. She closed her eyes, unable to bear the wash of emotion that poured through her. The last time she had heard it was

the night they had sat together in his big chair and so
nearly made love.

Why, oh, why had she let him stop? At least she
could have had that one night.

Now, perhaps, it was too late. He might not want
another man's leavings.

Dread closed her throat. Dear God, help me, she
prayed silently. Let him love me. Please, let him love
me.

CHAPTER TEN

THE fire had gone out, but he didn't feel cold. There was no room left for anything so trivial.

His mind strayed for the thousandth time, his imagination running riot. What were they doing? Had they gone up to their room yet? He glanced at his watch in the darkness, and swore softly. He couldn't see the time, but the clock in the hall had struck two some time ago.

Yes, of course they had. By now they were asleep, locked in each other's arms, their love reaffirmed.

The pain was almost physical.

He lay his head back against the chair and stared sightlessly across the room.

Tim had been difficult to settle. After he had put him to bed, the little boy had reappeared, his face drawn and thoughtful.

He had curled up on Andrew's knee in silence, and after a while he had started to talk about his mother and father.

'I suppose I should want them to get married again, shouldn't I?' he said very quietly, and Andrew's heart sank.

'Don't you?'

'Not really. I don't think she wants to. She's always sad after he goes, and she gets upset and crabby with him all the time.'

Andrew hugged him gently. 'People are often like

that with the people they love. It doesn't mean they don't want to be with them.'

Tim swivelled to look at him, his little face earnest. 'She's never like that with you. She's always smiley and happy — well, she was, anyway. Just the last few weeks she's been sad about you, too. Whenever I talk about you, she goes all misty and funny.'

Andrew felt a lump forming in his throat, and swallowed hard. He tried desperately for a more positive note. 'I thought you and your father were getting on better now?'

'We are — but I don't know about Mum. They laugh and have fun, and then he goes and I hear her crying in the night.'

'Maybe she just misses him.' Andrew had to choke the words out. 'I expect she just wants you all back together again. Maybe it will be all right now.'

'Maybe,' Tim said in a small voice, but he didn't sound convinced, and Andrew was unable to convince him. What could he say? He didn't believe it himself. All he knew was that she was lost to him, and the pain was almost more than he could bear.

He cleared his throat. 'Come on, young man, time for bed.'

'Will you read to me?'

Andrew looked down into his grey eyes, so like Jennifer's, and felt his heart contract.

'Of course I'll read to you. Come on.'

He took him back up, and they found Cadbury curled in a ball on the quilt.

'Can he sleep with me?' Tim asked anxiously as Andrew was leaving some time later.

He hesitated, then gave in. What harm could it do, this once?

'All right. Try and go to sleep now. If you want me, I'll either be downstairs or in my bedroom, OK?'

Tim nodded and snuggled down with the purring kitten, and Andrew left them, his heart heavy.

Poor kid. He was finding the situation very hard to take, and he wasn't alone. Andrew found the knowledge that Jennifer cried herself to sleep cut him to the quick. All he wanted was to make her happy, but he wouldn't get the chance.

He felt tears form in his eyes now, and flicked off the table lamp in the sitting-room. He didn't want Tim coming back down and catching him bawling his eyes out like a baby, but he didn't think he could hold on much longer.

He put on Fauré's *Requiem*, a masochistic choice with all the memories it brought, and, resting his head back, he closed his eyes and let the tears fall unheeded.

The back door was still unlocked, and Jennifer opened it slowly.

'Andrew?'

There was no sign of him in the kitchen, but she followed the music into the sitting-room. At first she thought he wasn't there, but then as her eyes adjusted to the dim light she saw him stretched out in his chair, his eyes closed.

She said his name again and he turned his head towards her, then sat up slowly.

'Jennifer?'

Her name was a hoarse whisper, more of a sigh than a word. She moved towards him.

'H-hi,' she faltered. 'It's only me.'

He stood up slowly and flicked on the light, blinking in the harsh glare. His eyes were red-rimmed and swollen, and his face was chalk-white. 'What is it? What's wrong?'

She took a deep breath, and the speech she had rehearsed flew straight out of her mind.

'I love you,' she said unevenly. 'I'm sorry I took so long to realise it, and I know you probably won't want me, but just on the off-chance that the offer's still open, I wanted you to know I'd be honoured to be your wife. . .'

He was silent, unmoving, and with a crushing sense of despair she realised she was right. He didn't want her. Oh, lord. . .

Her hands twisted together and she looked down, unable to look at him for fear of what she would see.

She heard him step towards her, felt the soft brush of his hands on her cheeks, and the slight pressure of his fingers under her chin tilting her face towards him.

'Jennifer,' he breathed, and then his arms were round her and she felt his chest heaving. 'Oh, my darling heart,' he said brokenly, and then there were no more words, only the feel of his arms safe around her and the ragged sound of his breathing. After an age he eased her away and looked down at her, and his eyes were filled with love.

'How could I not want you?' he murmured fervently. 'Don't you have any idea how much I love you?'

'I thought — you never said so —'

'Only because I felt it wasn't fair.'

She shook her head. 'Oh, Andrew, if only I'd known. . .'

'Well, you know now,' he told her shakily. 'There aren't words to tell you how much I love you.'

'Show me, then,' she whispered.

His eyes locked with hers, and the dark brown turned to smouldering coals. 'Are you sure? Because once I make love to you, I'll never let you go.'

'Is that a threat or a promise?' she asked with a trembling smile.

'A promise,' he vowed, and wordlessly he led her up the steep little stairs to his bedroom.

She heard the dull scrape of the lock, and remembered her son.

'Is Tim all right?'

Andrew smiled. 'He will be now. Come here.'

He undressed her slowly, his fingers shaking so badly that he could hardly make them co-operate. He stopped when he reached her underwear, and then stepped back, his eyes locked with hers, to peel off his own clothes.

Her breath caught as she watched him. He was so big—much bigger then she had realised, taller and broader and immensely powerful, and yet she felt no fear, only a trembling, incredulous joy. She reached out an unsteady hand and touched his chest, her fingers stroking the soft hair that clustered in the centre. His chest rose and fell sharply under her hand, and a dull flush lay on his cheeks. He wanted her.

Her hand shook, and he caught it in his, pressing it to his lips. 'Don't be afraid. I won't hurt you—I'll never hurt you.'

'I'm not afraid,' she told him, and looked up into his

warm, dark chocolate eyes—eyes that were filled with love.

He looked down at their hands. 'You've taken your ring off.'

'Yes. I gave it to Nick.'

'I don't want you getting pregnant,' he said almost harshly. 'Not now, not this weekend. When it happens, I want to be sure——'

He broke off, and realisation dawned.

'Oh, my darling. Do you really think I would have come to you from Nick's bed?'

He turned his head but he couldn't hide the shaft of pain that lanced through him.

Her fingers soothed his burning cheek. 'Let me tell you what happened.'

'No! Please, God, no. . .'

'When he kissed me——' Andrew sucked in a harsh breath and stiffened '—I shut my eyes and thought, if I pretended it was you, then maybe I would feel something.'

He looked back at her, his eyes like windows on his tortured soul. 'And?' he jerked out.

She smiled sadly. 'Nick realised what I was doing. He stopped, just before I stopped him. He told me to come to you. I didn't think I stood a chance, I didn't dare to hope that you loved me, but he told me I had to try.' She touched him again. 'I had nothing left to lose. Without you, I'm not whole any more. I can't live without you.'

Some of the strain left his face. 'All night,' he murmured, 'all night I've tortured myself. . .'

His hands came up and cupped her bare shoulders, and the warmth coursed through her, filling her with joy. 'I can't believe you're real,' he said softly. 'I've fantasised about this moment for so long, and I know damn well I'm going to blow it now it's here.'

She sighed and moved closer. 'You couldn't possibly blow it. All I want is for you to hold me.'

She felt the soft rumble of his laughter under her ear. 'Then you're going to get a hell of a shock.'

'Well, perhaps not all,' she said impishly, laughter bubbling in her eyes, and he lifted her and laid her carefully in the middle of the big, high bed.

'Where's Cadbury?' she asked.

He smiled slowly. 'With Tim — what a stroke of luck.'

She held out her arms, and he eased himself down beside her and gathered her against his chest, cradling her tenderly.

'I love you,' he whispered, his breath warm against her hair, and then he took her to paradise.

He woke her while it was still dark, and she went into the spare room — not because they wanted to deceive Tim, but because there was rather a lot for him to assimilate and they wanted to give him enough time.

Not, as Andrew said, that they expected any problems, and they were right.

He was obviously completely thrilled at the turn of events — largely, Andrew said drily, because he would have unlimited access now to seven cats, four bantams and the badgers' sett.

But there was more to it than that, and they all knew it.

He had only one reservation.

'I will still see Dad, won't I?' he asked them doubtfully.

'Oh, darling, of course. He's your father, and he always will be. Of course you'll see him, often. And Granny and Grandpa.'

'Only on condition he doesn't come back from them with any more kittens,' Andrew growled threateningly, and Tim, who was cuddling Cadbury at the time, giggled deliciously.

They set the date of the wedding provisionally for Christmas Eve, because it was Andrew's first day off as he was on call the next weekend.

'Can we get married on Christmas Eve?' Jennifer asked doubtfully.

'Dunno. I hope so — two weeks is longer than I want to wait as it is,' Andrew said with a groan. 'Ring the Register Office.'

She did, and they could, and so she arranged for them to go down to see the Registrar that day to book a time and make all the arrangements.

Later she rang Nick to tell him the news.

'Good,' he said simply. 'You deserve to be happy. I'm sorry I'm not the man for you, but I couldn't have chosen anyone I would trust more to care for you and my son.'

'Even though he's a stuffed shirt?' she teased.

He laughed ruefully. 'OK, I exaggerated. Anyway, if I'd been trying as hard as he was to hide my feelings, I guess I would have come over as a stuffed shirt. Give him my regards — when's the wedding? Perhaps I can return the favour and have Tim.'

'Christmas Eve.'

'Really? Great. I can take him to my parents — they'll love it.' He hesitated, something the old Nick would not have done, and then said, 'Is that OK? For me to have him for Christmas?'

'Oh, Nick, of course it's OK! Anyway, I expect Andrew will find me something to do — he's on call, so we'll probably be at the hospital for most of it.'

'How romantic!' he laughed.

The next fortnight seemed to fly and yet drag simultaneously. They were busy at the hospital, as usual, but the evenings when Andrew was on call were long and lonely, and the nights were harder still to bear.

Their last outpatients before the wedding was the cystic fibrosis clinic on the Thursday afternoon, and Jennifer was positively glowing.

'No second thoughts?' Andrew asked her as they paused briefly for tea, and she shook her head.

'Absolutely not. I've never done anything in my life before that has felt so positively right.'

His smile was warm and tender, but passion flickered in his eyes. 'Not long now,' he murmured.

'No — no, not long.'

There was a tap on the door and they jumped guiltily apart as Janet brought in a stack of notes.

She winked at them. 'Don't mind me — you two carry right on. It won't be the same after tomorrow.'

Andrew gave a wry groan after she had gone.

'If I hear one more joke. . .'

Jennifer grinned. 'I'm sure there'll be several. Shall I wheel in the next?'

'You'd better, before I forget my good intentions. Is it Jackie Long?'

'Mmm — her lung function's down a bit. I wonder how her knee is?'

'That's what I was wondering. Do you suppose

Michael Barrington would stroll over and have a look? He's only round the corner. If it's still playing up perhaps we need to be more aggressive so she can get back on her exercise programme.'

Jennifer laughed. 'Can you imagine what she'll be like with Michael? She was bad enough with Nick, and he hasn't sailed the Atlantic!'

Andrew grinned. 'Awful, I expect. Wheel her in, then.'

Jackie reported that her knee no longer hurt, although she was still resting it and exercising only with care and using her arms and trunk.

It felt cool, but before he advised her to resume her activities Andrew wanted to confer with an orthopaedic surgeon.

He rang the fracture clinic and spoke to Michael Barrington, who said he could easily pop over.

When he walked in, Jackie's reaction was predictably feminine and outrageous.

'Oh!' she simpered. 'You're the one who's been on the telly — gosh, you nearly *died*. That must have been *terrifying*.'

He grinned awkwardly. 'Actually it was just very cold and wet — and my head hurt where Clare hit me over the eye with the oar.'

'She what?' Andrew threw back his head and laughed. 'I thought you were wounded falling overboard.'

Michael chuckled. 'No such luck. Anyway, young lady, what can I do for you?'

The hem-hitching routine followed, and, like Nick, Michael ignored her flirtatious behaviour and concentrated on her knee.

'Well, it seems to have settled nicely. I would think

you could begin to introduce activities again, but nothing like Step Reebok — too demanding on that tendon. Avoid cycling and riding, as well, but otherwise play it by ear — try it, if it doesn't swell or get sore, try something else, but don't reintroduce everything at once. OK?'

She nodded, her lashes fluttering. 'Just one more thing — could I have your autograph?'

Michael flushed and demurred, but finally surrendered. 'As it's Christmas,' he said with an embarrassed grin, and Andrew handed him a piece of paper and watched, amused, as Jackie purred her thanks.

He escaped gratefully, and Andrew schooled his face and sent her off to see the physio for another barrage of exercises.

'Little madam,' he said to Jennifer afterwards.

'Just at the mercy of her hormones,' she said with a smile.

He snorted. 'Aren't we all?'

'One more day.'

His look almost singed her lashes off. 'Twenty and a half hours.'

She blinked. 'Really?'

He chuckled. 'Trust me — I've got a chart. I'm crossing every hour off.'

'Try Tim's trick,' she suggested. 'Go to bed early, then the night goes faster.'

'It needs to. Have we got everything arranged for tomorrow?'

She nodded. 'Yes. Just make sure you're there at one.'

'I will be — wild horses wouldn't keep me away.'

* * *

Nick collected her and Tim from the flat at twelve-thirty, his startling blue eyes looking suspiciously bright as he hugged her. 'You look beautiful,' he said huskily. 'He's a lucky man.'

Her eyes filled. 'Oh, Nick. . .'

'Shh. You'll wreck your make-up. Are you all ready?'

She nodded, checking her appearance again once more in the long mirror by the door. She was wearing a dove-grey suit with a cream silk shirt under it, and in the buttonhole was a creamy white rose from Andrew's garden. He had brought it to her last night and she had kept it in the fridge and this morning she had taped it to a little piece of fern snipped from one of her house plants.

Tim was looking smart, as well, in his school trousers and jacket with a new white shirt and a red tie. He had polished his shoes himself until they gleamed, and his case was ready by the door. For once, he looked surprisingly like his father, and Jennifer smiled mistily at them both.

'All set?' Nick asked, and she nodded.

'Can you manage Tim's Christmas presents as well?'

'Do we really need them?'

Tim gave his father a dry look, and Nick chuckled. 'I should think I can cope. Where are they?'

'Here. Don't drop the big one.'

He hefted it into his arms and groaned. 'What is it, bricks?'

She smiled. 'Just don't drop it.'

They made their way out to the car, and after loading all the presents and the case Nick settled Jennifer into the passenger seat, Tim into the back and then slid behind the wheel.

Before he started the car, he turned to her. 'You sure?'

She nodded, unable to stop the smile of happiness on her face. 'Yes, I'm sure.'

He winked. 'Let's go, then.'

It was a quiet wedding, with only a few friends in attendance. Jennifer's sister Sue, her only living relative, had been unable to come because she was extremely pregnant, but Andrew's brother was there, and the Barringtons, and Kathleen Hennessy and Jack Lawrence who were leaving for Ireland for their own wedding the day after Boxing Day.

Peter Travers, the other paediatrician, and his wife, and Maggie Bradshaw, the SHO on maternity leave, were also there. Ben, Maggie's husband, was unable to be there because he was holding the fort in A and E, but Janet, the outpatients receptionist, and Beattie, the domestic, were both there cheerleading.

After the short ceremony they all went back to the hospital canteen for an impromptu reception. Many of the guests had to return to duty, and as the crowd dwindled so Nick and Tim approached them.

'We're off,' Nick said. 'I'd like to get on the road before the crush really gets organised.'

'OK,' Jennifer replied. 'Take care of Tim, and have a lovely Christmas. We'll see you on Boxing Day.'

Nick nodded, then hugged her impulsively. Releasing her abruptly, he turned to Andrew and gripped his hand. 'Look after her. She's a very special woman.'

Andrew gave her a look that should have set her alight. 'I know,' he said softly. 'Don't worry, I'll take care of her.'

Then she kissed Tim goodbye, and watched them go, a thoughtful expression on her face.

'He still loves you,' Andrew said quietly.

'No. He just thinks he does. He'll be fine. Did you see the way he was trawling those nurses?'

Andrew chuckled. 'I wondered if you'd noticed.'

'Of course I noticed.' She looked up at him. 'What are we going to do now?'

He smiled ruefully. 'I can think of a thousand things, but one in particular comes to mind. Unfortunately, however, I think we're going to have to put our plans on hold. Anthony Craven's come in with a chest infection, and I want to pop up and see him, and then there's the carol service on the ward at six tonight. After that, though. . .'

The carol service was beautiful. One of their patients, a boy of eleven with a broken leg, was a chorister, and he led them in 'Once in Royal David's City', his voice soaring clear and pure around the ward. It was followed by all the old favourites, Andrew's wonderful, rich baritone blending with and balancing the higher voices of the children and the mothers and bringing a lump to Jennifer's throat so that she couldn't sing.

At the end of the service Andrew made his way round the ward, wishing all his patients a happy Christmas, and then, when they had shaken hands with all the staff and been deluged with good wishes, they slipped away and drove back to the cottage.

'I ought to have got some things from the flat,' she told him as they pulled up outside. 'I didn't think about it before.'

'You won't need anything,' he replied firmly. 'You can borrow my toothbrush, and clothes don't figure in my plans at all. You can get something tomorrow — or the next day.'

He led her into the sitting-room and revived the dying embers of the fire, then drew her into the centre of the room.

There was a sprig of mistletoe hanging from a beam, and he manoeuvred her underneath it with a smile.

'Merry Christmas, Mrs Barrett,' he said softly.

She felt choked with joy. 'Merry Christmas,' she whispered, and lifted her lips to his.

It was a devastating kiss, so full of tenderness and passion that she thought she would catch fire.

After a moment he lifted his head, and she read the question in his eyes.

She reached up and tugged on his tie.

'What are you doing?' he asked gruffly.

'Unwrapping my Christmas present. Want to join in?'

Laughter battled with need in his eyes, and then the need won.

'Oh, yes. . .'

Their clothes fell around them unheeded, and he drew her down in front of the fire.

'I love you,' he murmured, and as he took her in his arms the flames found an echo in his eyes.

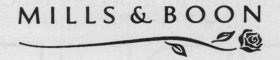

Discover the thrill of *Love on Call*
with 4 FREE Romances

FREE

BOOKS FOR YOU

In the exciting world of modern medicine, the emotions of true love acquire an added poignancy. Now you can experience these gripping stories of passion and pain, heartbreak and happiness - with Mills & Boon absolutely FREE! AND look forward to a regular supply of *Love on Call* delivered direct to your door.

❧ ❧ ❧

Turn the page for details of how to claim 4 FREE books AND 2 FREE gifts!

An irresistible offer from Mills & Boon

Here's a very special offer from Mills & Boon for you to become a regular reader of *Love on Call*. And we'd like to welcome you with 4 books, a cuddly teddy bear and a special mystery gift - absolutely FREE and without obligation!

Then, every month look forward to receiving 4 brand new *Love on Call* romances delivered direct to your door for only £1.80 each. Postage and packing is FREE!

Plus a FREE Newsletter featuring authors, competitions, special offers and lots more...

This invitation comes with no strings attached. You may cancel or suspend your subscription at any time and still keep your FREE books and gifts.

It's so easy. Send no money now but simply complete the coupon below and return it today to:

Mills & Boon Reader Service, FREEPOST, PO Box 236, Croydon, Surrey CR9 9EL.

— — — — — **NO STAMP NEEDED** — — — — ✂

YES! Please rush me 4 FREE *Love on Call* books and 2 FREE gifts! Please also reserve me a Reader Service subscription. If I decide to subscribe, I can look forward to receiving 4 brand new *Love on Call* books for only £7.20 every month - postage and packing FREE. If I choose not to subscribe, I shall write to you within 10 days and still keep the FREE books and gifts. I may cancel or suspend my subscription at any time simply be writing to you.
I am over 18 years of age.   Please write in BLOCK CAPITALS

Ms/Mrs/Miss/Mr _____ EP62D

Address _____

_____

_____ Postcode _____

Signature _____

mps MAILING PREFERENCE SERVICE